Echoes from the Attic

Richard Seltzer
and
Ethel Kaiden

Echoes from the Attic

Copyright © 2022 by Richard Seltzer and Ethel Kaiden

ISBN: 9798987129647

Library of Congress Control Number: 2022951332

Cover Design by All Things that Matter Press

Cover photo: Pexels

Published in 2022 by All Things that Matter Press

Acknowledgments

Richard thanks:

Rex Sexton for many years of encouragement and advice; Ardelle Cowie; Gay Walley; Claude Thau; my son Tim for reminding me how to tell a story; and my late wife Barbara for her infinite patience and brilliant insights.

Ethel thanks:

Children Shari and Jerry; Wendy and Joe; grandchildren Josh and Jessie, Eric, Ben and Bayley, Andrew and Alexis; and husband Chuck for being the best family on the planet. I would also like to thank my father Dr.Jack for letting me tag along as he brightened the world with brilliance and comedy.

Prologue ~ You Better Watch Out

The Back Bay, Boston, October 2008

As a freshman sharing an off-campus apartment with non-students, Patti felt no peer-pressure. On this summer-like October evening, she would wear an ankle-length dark-blue cotton dress that she had found in the attic and her Nike running shoes for comfort. It was a long walk from Fairfield Street to Tremont, and she wanted to enjoy it.

She was going out on her first real date since she started college with Ollie who had annoyed her so much when they first met that she dumped ice cubes down his pants.

They would stroll down Commonwealth Avenue like a couple in a Henry James novel, when the Back Bay had been newly reclaimed from the swamp, like Holland from the sea. She savored echoes from the past. She liked to believe that what we do now will matter in the future, as what happened in the past matters now.

It occurred to her that Ollie might wear his Tom Brady football jersey. That would make it difficult for her to maintain the mindset she wanted. She called Ollie on his cellphone and told him to wear a button shirt and a sports jacket, jeans, and sneakers.

She should be going out with her new apartment mate, Alex, instead of Ollie. It was just a week before Halloween, and Alex resembled Johnny Depp. She could have had him dress up as Captain Jack Sparrow and walk with a cautious sway to his step, prepared for threats from all directions. But tonight, she wanted to be in control. She knew exactly where she stood with Ollie, but Alex was unpredictable, both intriguing and unsettling.

Earrings? she wondered, looking in the mirror. Yes, of course. The magic ones Alex gave her. She would feel naked without them.

A week before, on the way back from BU on Commonwealth Avenue near the intersection with Massachusetts, first Alex, then Patti had noticed that someone was following them, keeping half a block behind, but not trying to hide. Tall, wearing a dark raincoat, despite the clear sky.

If this were a scene in a movie, Patti would have guessed this guy had some shady connection with Alex and wanted to intimidate him.

Alex had insisted that no one had it in for him, but Patti never knew when Alex was telling the truth. She thought of him as a computer geek with a devilish imagination. She guessed he sometimes walked on the dark side.

Alex made her promise not to tell their apartment mates Marge and Tom about the stalker because they would worry like parents, and that wouldn't help anyone. She readily agreed, knowing that secrets bind, and she might enjoy feeling bound to him, if not too tightly.

The next day, he gave her a wireless headset in the form of earrings that connected to a cell phone she kept in her pocket.

"Just press the speed dial to connect to me. Then you can speak to me and hear me without others suspecting, and I can hear everything that's going on around you."

He had the same kind of headset embedded in his Red Sox cap.

"So now you can tell me answers to questions in class," she suggested.

"Better still, we can have phone sex anywhere, anytime," he joked.

The gold-stud earrings went well with her short bouncy blond hair. She would have worn them often just for the look. And, new to the city, she needed the sense of security they gave her, to keep fear of the unknown at a manageable, but titillating distance.

She shouldn't have had sex with Alex—not yet. Yes, she enjoyed hanging out with him and was attracted to him. She had been curious and impulsive that one time. But as apartment mates they saw each other every day. And the intimate way he looked at her now made her feel uncomfortable. She wasn't ready for a relationship with anyone, not yet. She didn't want to feel that she belonged to him or to anyone else. That's why she had said yes to Ollie for this date. Doing so signaled that she could go out with whoever she wanted. But at the same time, she liked the sexual tension with Alex and didn't want that to go away. And keeping their mutual attraction secret from Marge and Tom gave a buzz of the forbidden to their continuing flirtation.

Ollie was good as eye candy, but she wasn't attracted to football-player types; and she and Alex had joked repeatedly about the ice cube incident in her first encounter with Ollie.

Tonight, Ollie met her at her apartment, dressed as ordered. He cleaned up well. He looked shell-shocked, like he had when she agreed to go out with him. That adoring look of his made him the perfect accessory for tonight—his attention to her was like a spotlight shining on her and her alone.

This night was a celebration of herself—a teenager from small-town New Hampshire, coming of age in the big city. Her trip to Europe last summer had been a rehearsal. This was opening night.

She liked the feel of Ollie's shoulder against her cheek. She luxuriated in his physical presence. She enjoyed the image of herself with him, turning heads as she walked down Commonwealth like a model on a runway. Some day she would look back on this night and cringe remembering how shallow she was. But right now—eighteen and gorgeous and knowing it—let the good times roll.

They crossed the Public Gardens, then the Boston Common. Once they got to the Loew's theater complex, she ducked into the ladies' room and, using her magic earrings, warned Alex off.

"Look, Alex. I know you're following me. I spotted you a block away. Back off, please. I'm just going to a movie. Yes, Ollie was a jerk before. But tonight, he's sober and polite. Cool it. Just let me be."

Alex didn't answer, but she could hear street traffic through the earrings. He was outside, and he didn't deny he had been following her.

After the movie got out, when Ollie and Patti were crossing the Common again, they went through a dark spot. It was a moonless night. There were no other pedestrians in sight. The lights had been on earlier. Why would half a dozen bulbs go out at once? Patti held tight to Ollie's arm.

Something moved off to the right.

A homeless man was stretched out on a park bench, covered with a blanket.

Patti gripped so tight that Ollie shook her off in pain.

At that moment, a knife blade flashed between them.

Ollie and Patti both ran.

The assailant tackled Patti.

Ollie kept running.

Patti had the wind knocked out of her.

By the time she was able to get enough air in her lungs to scream, the assailant was on top of her, pinning her arms to the ground with his knees. He had the knife to her throat. She didn't dare scream.

Through her earrings, she heard Alex's heavy breathing as he started to run to the rescue. He said he was near Arlington Street. He could get to her in less than five minutes. She had to talk to the guy, keep him off balance, make him think rather than act.

Fortunately, the assailant seemed to be in no hurry. He seemed to be savoring the moment, enjoying her fear and his power over her.

"911?" she whispered.

"No time," Alex answered. "If I disconnect to call them, I'll lose my connection to you. I'll be there quicker than I could explain things to the cops. Hang on."

"Help," she whispered back.

"No one's going to help you," the assailant assured her, rubbing the side of the blade along her throat.

"Tell him you're a cop," Alex coached her. "Tell him that these earrings are transponders, and the cops are listening and recording."

"I'm wired," she said out loud. "I'm an undercover cop. You're under arrest."

"Sure, and I'm Santa Claus."

"These earrings are transponders."

"And this knife is an atomic bomb."

"Put your head close to an earring."

"Certainly, my love."

Alex shouted. "You're under arrest! Drop that knife or I'll order my men to fire."

"What the hell?" he shouted, pulling his head back, as if burnt. "Is that a web cam thing? A web cam even out here?"

Alex told her, "The guy is nuts. Tell him yes. Web cams seem to spook him more than your being wired. Go with it. I'm running as fast as I can. I'm crossing Charles Street. I'm just a minute away. Talk up the web cam thing."

"Yes, a web cam," she insisted. "Lots of web cams. The trees, the lamp posts are full of web cams. You're live on the Internet."

"God! Web cams everywhere!"

Freaked, the guy ran, shouting back at her, "Go to hell you green-haired bitch."

Alex arrived moments later, helped her to Beacon Street, and called a cab with his cell phone. Physically, she seemed fine except for a few scratches. But emotionally she was shattered.

"He wasn't a homeless bum," she insisted, talking rapidly and nonstop all the way home. "This guy was dressed in ordinary clothes. He didn't smell of alcohol. His hands weren't calloused. He's probably some everyday office worker. He was obsessed with web cams. And he knew I had dyed my hair green earlier today. He knew me. I wasn't just some random victim. He had seen me before. He had seen me when I had green hair. But I only had green hair in the apartment. He saw me in the apartment. He knew I'd be here in the Common coming and going from the movie—right here, right now. I talked to Ollie about the date from a cell phone in the apartment. I mentioned what movie and what time. I mentioned that since it was such a beautiful night, we could walk all the way and that I liked the look of the Common all lit up at night, that I like to walk by the wading pool. He heard all that. He was waiting for me."

1 ~ Loose Lips

Five weeks earlier, end of August 2008

If the woman hadn't died, if Tom hadn't seen her die, if he hadn't felt responsible for her death, he wouldn't have spoken to the stranger, cutting short the sequence of events that disrupted his life and the lives of Marge and Patti and Alex.

Tom was sitting near the front window at Flanagan's a few steps down from street-level, on Newbury Street in Boston. He was at the vintage end of Flanagan's with 1920s hand-carved mahogany molding and a long mirror behind the bar, like a scene out of *The Great Gatsby*. And at the other end of the room, a very different crowd was gathered around a huge flat screen showing a Celtics game.

A tall stranger in a battered straw Red Sox hat approached him, and Tom turned away to look out the window, signaling that he didn't want to be disturbed.

Tom looked at the first-floor shops across the street; at the dark-stone Victorian homes above them. They had fairy-tale rooftops with parapets, gabled windows and, above them stood the soaring massive Prudential Center and John Hancock Tower. The Boston of today, yesterday, and tomorrow, one on top of the other.

On the sidewalk across the street, he saw a woman holding a map. She was wearing a Statue-of-Liberty shirt that only a foreigner would wear, and a skirt with a slit up the side that showed off her long legs. She nearly collided, repeatedly, with oncoming pedestrians, who veered to their right while she went to her left. "British tourist," Tom concluded. Next he thought, *It's a good thing she isn't driving*. He imagined her newly divorced, off on her own for the first time.

He remembered when he was in London with Diane, then his wife, now his ex. He had nearly stepped in front of a speeding taxi, and she pulled him back. If he had been alone, if they had been divorced then, she wouldn't have been there to save him.

Then the tourist stopped, looked to her left, as if forcing herself to remember that she was in America and cars driving on the right side of the street would come from that direction. But this was Newbury Street, a one-way street, and the traffic came from the other direction.

He wanted to warn her but hesitated because she spread out her map on the hood of a car. Maybe he was reading too much into what he saw, and she had no intention of crossing the street, or could do so safely, as thousands of tourists do every day in Boston. Besides, the stranger in the straw Red Sox hat was standing between him and the door.

Then he made eye contact with Tracy, the new very blond waitress, through the mirror behind the bar. Or rather, she made eye contact with him. Hers was a laser look, like she wanted to talk to him. He smiled, and she started maneuvering toward him through the crowd. He sat back down and finished his beer.

He was probably misinterpreting Tracy, like he was misinterpreting that British tourist.

Tracy was probably signaling somebody else. And the Brit outside with the map probably wasn't divorced. If he tried to warn her about the traffic, she would turn away, presuming this was just a pick-up line; and maybe it was. He felt untethered—no wife, no job—blown this way and that by random circumstance and whim. With no one depending on him anymore, he didn't know who he was.

Besides, he had always been awkward when trying to meet women. Back in college he often put on a tough-guy act, which back-fired badly. Only by chance, having several of the same classes, and getting into the habit of walking together from one class to the other, did Diane get to see beyond that tough-guy cover identity to the vulnerable and caring person she fell in love with and married, his softer inner self that he lost during many years of work-a-day habit. The world was too much with him, and now his wife and kids weren't with him at all.

Now after he'd been out of circulation for twenty-five years of marriage, attractive available women made him feel insecure, hesitant, and self-conscious. The more attractive the worse his reaction. And Tracy was over-the-top gorgeous.

In case she was heading his way, he tried to mold his face into a confident, cool expression. He stroked the scar below his lower lip. An image of Long John Silver—Robert Newton in the Disney version of *Treasure Island*—flashed through his mind.

When he had first seen Tracy a week ago, he had dismissed her as a kid, just above drinking age. She was great to look at with her bare midriff, low-slung jeans, and belly-button ring, but she wasn't someone he could take seriously or who would be likely to have any interest in him. She was fantasy in the flesh.

Then Bill the bartender had told him that Tracy was older and more serious than she looked. She was over thirty, a divorcee, a former English teacher from Kansas who had come east for a fresh start. But even when he considered her as an adult, he continued to be uncomfortable around her because with her looks, she was in a different league where he couldn't compete. He didn't flirt with her or try to get to know her. He just enjoyed watching her from a distance.

Now she adroitly navigated through the crowd and reached him as he was finishing his beer.

"Hi, Tom. *Sam Adams*?" she asked, putting a new glass down in front of him.

He nodded, pleased that she remembered both his name and his brand. She seemed to be inviting conversation. He cleared his throat but before he could say a word, she had moved away.

Just then, out of the corner of his eye, he saw the British tourist fold up her map, and step off the curb. Once again, she looked to the left, while a taxi was coming at her from the right.

Tom jumped to his feet, shouldered his way past the guy with the Red Sox hat, and sprinted toward the door.

Then his left leg went stiff. It wouldn't bend. He hobbled and limped, but still he kept his balance.

Before he reached the sidewalk, he heard the crash. By the time he got to the street, a crowd was already gathering around the body. Someone checked her pulse and shook his head. Several people talked into cell phones. In less than a minute, sirens sounded in the distance.

Tom stumbled back into Flanagan's and collapsed into his seat.

Tracy was standing at the nearby window, watching the aftermath. "She isn't ..." she asked Tom.

"Yes, she is."

"Did you know her?"

"No. But I could see it was going to happen. I could have warned her and stopped her."

"And your leg?" Tracy asked. "Is your leg okay?"

"Fine. Perfectly fine."

"Well, why that sudden limp?"

Tom cringed with embarrassment. "Maybe someday I'll tell you about it."

He shut his eyes and took a deep breath. A minute or two passed. Then Tracy was gone again, and the tall stranger was sitting next to him.

Under normal circumstances, Tom would have moved to another, less-populated part of the room. He preferred to drink alone or with people he knew well. He would never start talking to a stranger, even one like this, with a Jacoby Ellsbury Red Sox Jersey and an old Mitt Romney campaign button—dressed as if inviting conversation about baseball or argument about politics.

Without that woman's death, they would have never talked. And if they had never talked, this would be a very different story.

"Easy does it. Easy does it," the stranger intoned with a western twang. "It wasn't your fault. It wasn't your destiny to stop it."

"As if I have a destiny."

"You are who you are. You are what you come from. That's what matters. That's the signal, the message. The rest is just accidents and random noise. There's far too much random noise in cities. So many people without anchors, without responsibility, just drifting. You only really live if people depend on you; if what you do matters. It's not easy to find the true path in all the city noise. But it's there for those who seek it, thank the Lord."

Pieces of what this stranger said rang true, but Tom was in no mood to sort out the meaning of life in general, or the meaninglessness of his own life. Tom tuned out the insistent, self-assured voice of this stranger, focusing instead on the image of the British tourist extending her long shapely leg and stepping into the street—her floppy green hat, a glitter of earrings. It was as if he had taken a series of digital photos, and the album of them kept playing and replaying, and he couldn't turn it off.

As the ambulance started to drive away—slow and silent—Tom was surprised to hear the stranger still droning on. He took a last, deep swallow of his *Sam Adams*, and Tracy materialized with another glass of it.

She smiled warmly, as if they were old friends, and said, "Don't leave tonight before I have a chance to talk to you."

Tom hoped he didn't look as shocked as he felt.

"Bill says you have a room for rent," she explained. "He showed me the ad in the paper. That might be just what I'm looking for."

She turned and dashed away before he started choking. He hoped she hadn't noticed.

The stranger gave Tom a helpful whack on the back, and he regained his composure.

"Is that a problem?" the stranger asked.

"I rented that room two days ago," Tom admitted. "In fact, I took on three new boarders. What timing."

"Well, can't you change your mind?"

"No way. The four of us have been working around the clock, changing things so we can all fit in. If she had asked me before, no problem. But there's nothing I can do now."

"That waitress is a looker. You don't meet somebody like that very often. Maybe you could come up with some excuse and get rid of those new roommates of yours. If it was me, I'd be tempted."

"No. I couldn't. You couldn't either if you knew those boarders."

"Then you know them well?"

"Well enough. We went from strangers to friends in a few hours. They really need the place. I couldn't let them down. I'm not that kind of person."

"Are they guys like yourself? Buddies you'd like to hang out with?"

"No. One's a professional woman, a little older than that waitress. Then there's another girl, a college freshman, and a guy about college age, but off on his own, some kind of techno-whiz."

"And just like that, you feel an obligation to them? I guess I don't understand city ways. Where I come from there aren't many folks, and we all know one another. We all grew up together and went to school with one another and go to church with one another. We trust one another. We'd do anything for one another. But outsiders—that's different. It takes years to build a bond with them. Only way you trust them is if you've got a contract with them, and that better be written, clear and binding. Do they have a contract with you?"

"No. They're just renting rooms in my apartment. There's no lease. But I gave my word."

"I must say it's refreshing to hear you say that—unaccountable but refreshing. Here I'm talking about old-time values; and you're the one that's living by them. Ironic. Maybe this rough and tough image of the random violent city is just the surface and underneath you find moral sensitivity and bonds of human fellowship of a kind I'd never have imagined."

"But the random violence is real, too," Tom admitted. "When I was showing Marge, the older woman, around my apartment for the first time, going up the ladder to the attic, I saw the place had been broken into. Somebody had broken a hole in the window above the latch. A couple of boxes were missing from the hallway—probably old plate-silver bowls and serving dishes. Stuff I never used."

"I can imagine the fear you must have felt, realizing that thieves could break in at any time."

"Fear? No. I felt embarrassed. I asked her, the would-be boarder, to wait a minute while I cleared a path through the boxes. I opened the window wide so she wouldn't see the hole. With my foot, I pushed the broken glass under the rug. Fortunately, she didn't notice."

"And what did you do about the break-in? Did you report it to the police?"

"No way. It was no big deal."

"Well, what did you do to stop the guy from coming back?"

"Back? There must be hundreds of attics like mine in downtown Boston—easy to get in and swipe antique stuff the owners would never miss. Just go from roof to roof and get in through the windows. I have no idea when they hit my place. I was the random victim of a somebody's burglary business. I've lived in the city my whole life. Randomness I can live with. It's violence targeted at me as an individual that would scare me."

"So did you put bars on your windows? Or install an electronic security system?"

"There's no way I'd go to that kind of trouble and expense. And I didn't want to spook the new tenants. I just put stickers on the attic windows saying the place is electronically protected and monitored. I bought the stickers over the Internet."

"So, your place isn't protected?"

"Of course not. If burglars were targeting my place, nothing would stop them. But for random burglary, the stickers are all I need to scare them away. Guys like that have plenty of targets to choose from. They won't take unnecessary risks."

"I wonder if your tenants would think the same."

"What they don't know—"

"Have you always taken in boarders?"

"No. I'm a rookie landlord."

"Married?"

"My divorce became final six months ago."

"Kids?"

"Two—Mark and Laurel. Both grown up and moved out."

"It must be hard living alone."

"I got so used to the non-stop noise that when they were gone, at first I left the TV and music on, not to listen, just to drive away the silence. I stopped doing that about a month ago. Now I'm taking in boarders, and I have to get used to living with three strangers."

"So you own the place?"

"I own the entire building. It's been in my family for three generations."

"Three generations, you say? I never met a real Boston Brahmin before. Old Back-Bay. Old wealth. The opposite of easy-come easy-go. You look like you grew up with money and take it for granted."

Tom had never thought of himself that way and liked the sound of it. So he didn't correct the impression—didn't mention the divorce settlement and the fact that he had been laid off, that all he had was occasional contract work, and that his financial straits had forced him to take in boarders. He decided not to contradict this stranger's unwarranted admiration.

"So this is a social thing for you," the stranger concluded. "The building belongs to you, and still you take in boarders in your own apartment. Are the girls lookers?"

"Definitely. Patti, the freshman reminds me of Reece Witherspoon in *Legally Blond*. Imagine Tracy, the waitress here, more than ten years younger. Blond like Tracy, only wide-eyed and enthusiastic about every detail of her new, independent life. As for Marge, she's a pleasure to look at, too, but she has such a take-charge commanding presence you don't notice her looks at first. She's a powerhouse."

"Powerhouse? You mean pushy and controlling?"

"No, I mean that meeting her for the first time was like hitting a force field."

"And that turns you off?" the stranger prompted.

"That question is in the wrong ballpark. She's a mature and intriguing woman. Getting to know her well could be both a challenge and an adventure. There's something about the way her mind works, the way her words get me thinking and talking. It's like I've been sleepwalking ever since my wife left me, and meeting Marge was like stepping into a cold shower on a hot day. It was both shocking and refreshing. I could imagine staying up all night with Marge, just talking, and that being an incredible high."

"Is that something you do often—talk all night to a beautiful woman and never get to first base?"

"No. That's never happened to me. But with her I could imagine it."

"This knock-out brunette and the young one, the knock-out blond ..."

Tom looked up and saw Tracy staring at him and smiling, as if she had overheard and thought they were talking about her. And the stranger turned quickly following his eyes. In so doing, his top shirt button came loose, revealing that under the Red Sox jersey, this guy was wearing a well-ironed white shirt and a, like he had a habit of formal dress and found it difficult to dress down deliberately. Tom suddenly realized that this guy was too clean shaven, his hair too neatly combed, he was altogether too well groomed—like a Jehovah Witness or Mormon missionary. This guy wasn't who he was pretending to be. He wasn't to be trusted.

"What was that?" Tom asked, defenses on alert.

"Where do they come from—the brunette and the blond? Do they have family or close friends nearby?"

"Wait a minute. I didn't say anything about Marge's hair color."

"You must have."

"No way. What are you after, mister?" Tom fired back. "Who are you, anyway? I don't even know your name."

"Easy does it. Easy does it, buddy. No need to get defensive. Remember, those women are strangers to you. You don't know them, any better than you know me." The stranger got up abruptly and left.

"What's your name, mister?" Tom called after him. The stranger ignored him, merging with the pedestrian traffic outside.

Tom left, too, avoiding Tracy. He didn't know what to tell her.

He headed away from the scene of the accident, over to Boylston Street, for a large black coffee at Dunkin Donuts. Then he walked straight home, crossing streets only at crosswalks with walk lights, and looking in all directions, checking for traffic and for a tall man in an old straw Red Sox hat.

Maybe he had mentioned Marge's hair color. Or maybe the guy had just guessed. That's not difficult since men recognize so few colors— blond, brunette, redhead. Women see differently. Like Eskimos and snow, he had told Diane, in defense of his ignorance. Diane would take ten or fifteen minutes staring at the hundreds of choices at CVS. She tried a new shade of hair color every month. And she was unforgiving when he didn't notice the difference.

But something about that guy was wrong, very wrong. If his knowing Marge's hair color hadn't triggered danger, it would have been the tone of his voice, or odor of sweat. That guy was nervous. For him, their conversation wasn't casual. Their sharing a table at Flanagan's wasn't random. Nothing about that guy was random. He was deliberate, premeditated. He was too curious about Tom's apartment and the break-in and the lack of security.

Still, Tom was over-reacting—mad at himself for talking too freely to a common stranger and taking that anger out on the other guy. He wasn't his usual self tonight—the sexy British tourist hit by a cab and dying right in front of him, and then Tracy wanting to rent his room. His head was spinning, and not just now. He hadn't recovered yet from the shock of Marge showing up at his door, at dawn two days ago.

2 ~ Room for Rent

A few days before that

The morning when Tom first met Marge, he woke up abruptly on the mattress on the floor of his bed-less bedroom. Ambulance sirens. Gusting wind rattling the windows. Daylight. The alarm clock hadn't gone off. He hadn't needed the alarm since he lost his job.

What woke him was the old-fashioned ring of a land-line telephone. It must be Diane, no one else used that number. Just let it ring.

No, maybe it was about a job—another short-term project or maybe a shot at something permanent. He had sent his resume dozens of places.

He scrambled off the mattress and, in the corner of the room under a shirt, he found the phone just in time to pick it up before it switched to voicemail.

"Hello?" He asked tentatively.

"Hello," replied a female voice, with a western or southern twang. "Sorry to call so early, but rooms are hard to find in the Back Bay. I wanted to reach you before anyone else."

"Rooms? Yes, my ad. You must have seen my ad. But how could you have seen it?" he continued. "It hasn't been printed yet."

"It's online. I'm reading it on my iPhone. Can I stop by now and have a look?"

He sat back down on the mattress to get his bearings. "How long will it take you to get to Fairfield Street?" he asked, calculating he needed an hour to get dressed, drink coffee, and straighten up.

"I'm standing in the lobby."

"But the ad just gave the street, not the full address."

"And how many buildings on Fairfield have a room-for-rent sign this time of year?"

"But the place is a mess," he pleaded.

"Just buzz me in," she continued. "You're on the fourth floor, right?"

"Wait a minute. This is too fast." He carried the phone back into the kitchen, nearly stumbling on the long cord.

"Please. The city is flooded with incoming students. The only rooms available are out in the suburbs. If I'm lucky enough to be the first to call, give me a chance. Buzz me in."

"Okay, already." He dropped the phone on the counter; found his jeans and an old tee-shirt on the kitchen floor; and awkwardly pulled them on. Then he turned on the faucet and splashed cold water on his face before finally hitting the buzzer.

By the time he opened the door to his apartment, the woman was already on the third floor. Looking down the stairwell, he admired her figure and how fast she raced up the stairs.

"You're not even winded," he noted as she reached his door.

"I try to stay in shape."

"So you don't mind that the apartment is this high and that there's no elevator?"

"It's good exercise."

She was wearing a tartan skirt, white blouse, and a scarf that matched the skirt. He was surprised to find himself paying attention to her clothes, trying to describe her clothes to himself, avoiding looking her in the eye, like avoiding looking directly at the sun. He felt disoriented, demoted to uncouth, little-kid status, like when he tried to learn the rudiments of Italian for a business trip and the words that the CD gave as English for articles of women's clothing were all foreign to him.

Her hair was light brown, probably dyed. He could tell that much. Diane would know the Clairol number and the fancy name.

She was almost as tall as Tom, who was five eleven.

Her face reminded him of Meg Ryan. Her physique … he forced himself not to stare. From the smile on her face, he must have been staring, and not at her face.

Finally, she broke the silence, "Marge. Marge Manchester." She reached out and shook his hand, which was limp.

It took him a moment to remember his own name and respond, "Tom Case."

Marge glanced beyond him at the kitchen/dining room. In the middle of the room stood a table consisting of a door resting on boxes. An open laptop was on the table, with unopened mail, and *The Boston Globe* open to a half-finished Sudoku puzzle. The kitchen wastebasket was full of pizza boxes, and McDonald's and Burger King wrappings. Nearby lay a plastic trash bag full of empty Coke cans.

He muttered excuses, "Diane, my ex-wife, took the furniture. And the mess ... I figured I'd have another day before the ad ran. Would you like to come back later?"

"No. It's better this way. If I rent this room of yours, you won't be on your best behavior all the time. It's better that I see the place in its natural state. That'll give me a better idea of what to expect."

"So, the mess doesn't gross you out?"

"Honesty never grosses me out."

He realized that, caught off guard, he was acting "natural," rather than putting on a tough-guy pose. Yes, he was awkward and inarticulate. But maybe she'd see that as vulnerable and honest. The way she strode and looked around, she liked the place, and maybe him, too, just the way they were. He was tempted to go overboard with honesty—telling her that he had been laid off after his wife left him, that he had been a principal software engineer, and his job was exported to India. But before he could decide to start, she was walking through the apartment on her own.

He left well-enough alone and microwaved a couple mugs of coffee. From a folding chair by the make-shift kitchen table, he glimpsed her as she passed doorways.

It was seven o'clock in the morning, an outrageous time for a stranger to ring your doorbell. But what a stranger. He had never imagined that an attractive, mature woman might answer his ad. If he had met Marge anywhere else, he would have wanted to strike up a conversation. But here she was in his apartment already. What could he say to her? How could he play landlord to someone like her? None of the questions he had imagined asking made sense now. Despite his better judgment, he was far more concerned about making a good impression on her than interviewing her as a potential tenant.

She started back through the rooms for a second time. Maybe she felt as awkward as he did. He poured himself a second cup of coffee and reheated the cup meant for her.

***

Marge had been delighted that Tom, unlike most people who place classified ads, had included his full name. That made it easier for her to check his background on the Web. A Google search had shown that he was a software engineer, an MIT grad, and married. From his MIT class, she figured he was about forty-five and guessed his children had grown up and moved out, and he and his wife wanted to get extra income from a spare bedroom. It would be a simple business proposition—she needed a room; he and his wife needed the money. So long as they were reasonable people and kept to themselves, they could get along fine. The place was just a few blocks from her work. But something felt wrong to her.

On the way here—crossing Boylston St. near the Hynes Center, heading down Fairfield St. toward Commonwealth, the old stone buildings on both sides of the street had loomed ominously, blocking the rising sun. She had stopped and looked around, twice, three times. She sensed that someone was following her, but she didn't see anyone. She was over-anxious about getting this room. Maybe that made her jumpy. Or maybe she was stressed from three weeks sharing a studio apartment with a friend, not getting much sleep on the sofa. When she met the landlord, she didn't want to come across as desperate. She took deep breaths. No one would be lurking in shadows at seven in the morning on a busy Back Bay street. She was rational and logical to a fault. She never let intuition interfere with her decision making.

When she heard his deep voice on the intercom, she checked her pocketbook. Yes, she had remembered the pepper spray.

At the door, when he mentioned his ex, at first she didn't register the meaning. She was so concerned about making a good first impression that she didn't pay close attention to his words. And his winning smile and deep voice put her off her guard. By the time she realized that he was divorced and living alone, she was already in the kitchen.

He wasn't bad looking, even unshaven and with rumpled hair. He came across as candid, spontaneous, and sensitive, but still wounded and disoriented by the breakup of his marriage. She wished she had met him in another context.

She glanced at the laptop computer on the makeshift kitchen table. The screensaver was a sequence of family photos, probably from Cape Cod, taken maybe twenty years ago. Caught in awkward poses, laughing at himself, she saw signs of the same self-conscious vulnerability she saw today. From what she had found using Google, she had expected him to be middle-aged, solid, and dependable. Now she sensed another side of him—lingering innocence and naivete and expectation.

Marge accidentally moved the mouse, and the solitaire card game Free Cell appeared. When stressed, she also played that game over and over again. And here he was opening his place to her, in its "natural" state. It would be awkward and impolite not to give it a thorough look.

The apartment consisted of a combination kitchen and dining room, a living room, and three bedrooms. The kitchen/dining room had doorways to the other four rooms, and to the one bathroom.

In what must be his bedroom, she saw a mattress on the floor, and three baskets of unwashed laundry.

In what was probably his daughter's room, which was the room for rent, the walls were pink, and there was a box of dolls in the corner.

The bathroom was small, with no towels. The toothpaste tube had no top. The toilet dripped, and the seat was up. The toilet paper dispenser was empty. An economy pack of Charmin toilet paper was open, and the rolls scattered on the floor. In the medicine cabinet she saw half a dozen boxes of hair color, probably left by his ex.

His office had floor-to-ceiling shelves stuffed with books. Boxes of computer peripherals and software and manuals lay in the middle of the floor. A desktop computer with a flat screen monitor sat on the desk. This computer, too, was on. It had probably been left on all night. The screen saver was another sequence of photos—probably from his daughter's wedding. She moved the mouse, and once again Free Cell appeared on the screen.

The furnishings in the living room consisted of a beanbag chair and a large flat-screen TV, tuned to CNN Headline News, with the audio muted.

After walking through all the rooms once, she felt ambivalent. The ceiling-to-floor windows made the place bright, and the lack of furniture made the rooms seem spacious. Apparently, he had nothing to hide. She sensed he'd be easy to get along with. She would have grabbed the room, right away, if she'd be moving in with a married couple. But with a single guy, the arrangement might lead to emotional complications—a mess it would be hard to get out of.

She walked back through all the rooms, slowly. The more she looked, the more she liked. But still she didn't think she'd take it, even if he wanted her to, which wasn't at all certain.

Finally, she sat down across from him at the kitchen table.

"You might consider buying some furniture," she suggested.

"Yes, I've been meaning to get around to that."

"How long ago did your wife move out?"

"A year and a half. The divorce took a year to finalize. It's been a difficult time."

"I can imagine."

"What do you think of the place?" Tom asked, handing her a big mug of steaming-hot coffee.

"It's amazing," she admitted, with a wide grin. "I grew up in a big old house built around the same time as this."

Silently, she sipped her coffee. She was relieved that he didn't say anything more, giving her a chance to sort through her thoughts. She liked his blue-green eyes. She liked the unassuming way he leaned back, balancing his chair on its back legs, and resting one hand on top of the other, near the knob of the door that now served as a table.

She admitted to herself that she was attracted to Tom and sensed his attraction to her. And this was a perfect location. But she knew she couldn't have it both ways. If she got the room, he would become her landlord and romance would be out of the question. She'd have to make sure he understood that, without explicitly saying so.

Marge took three large swallows of the coffee, then broke the silence, "The room is certainly big enough and the location is great. But I don't think this can work."

"Why?"

She hesitated. She didn't want to blurt out that up until a few weeks ago she had lived with a man she had expected to marry, that he had started acting jealous and suspicious, for no reason, and that now she was sleeping on a friend's couch.

Instead, she explained, "I need a place to stay for a year or two while I put my life back together. And here you are just a few blocks from where I work. And this fine old building, with its Victorian woodwork and tall ceilings, reminds me of the house I grew up in back in northern Arizona, near the Grand Canyon and Utah. I come from a big Mormon family. But I have lots of stuff I haul around with me from one place to the next, that I don't really need but can't get rid of. I shouldn't be looking for just a room, but rather part of a house, with a big storage area in the basement or attic."

"This place has an attic," he announced with evident delight.

"I couldn't tell from the street. Do you have rights to attic space?"

"All of it."

"Show me."

From a nearby shelf, he grabbed a long pole, with a hook on the end, and triggered a latch in the ceiling. A trap door opened, and a ladder came down. He gestured for her to climb up first. She declined. She didn't want this stranger, who might become her landlord, tempted to look up her skirt.

Climbing the ladder, she slipped a hand inside her pocketbook and confirmed again that the pepper spray was there.

He seemed like a great guy, and the many references to him on the Web confirmed that opinion. But she had just met him. What if his wife had left him for good reason? What if, despite his surface normality, he was a drug addict, or had a violent temper? She paused, took a deep breath, and left the latch of her pocketbook open.

When her head broke the plane of the attic floor, sparkles reflected at her from all sides. Fragments of broken glass. He was scrambling to hide a mess. A broken window. Storm damage? Unlikely. No trees around. A break-in, probably. And he didn't want her to know. And she didn't want him to know she knew.

She interpreted that he wanted to protect her, not just from danger but from the fear of danger. And his own fear, which he tried to mask, wasn't of burglars, but rather that she might be scared away by such a possibility. It wasn't just that he wanted to rent a room, but rather that he wanted her to be the one to take it. And his restrained, self-conscious, boyish attraction to her, attracted her to him.

To distract him, so he wouldn't see that she saw, Marge pretended to stumble against an upright piano in the hall. Tom rushed to catch her, and she signaled that she was okay—no need for physical contact. She didn't want physical contact. She needed to deal with this decision rationally.

Reorienting herself, she was delighted with what she saw—bright light from the huge window cast shadows and mystery among the partitions, trunks, and boxes. Before he could follow her eye to the broken pane near the latch, she blurted out, "How did you get a piano up here?"

"I have no idea," he chuckled, evidently relieved that that was what she wanted to ask about. "That was long before my time. I don't think anyone has played it for twenty years or more. It would cost far more than it's worth to get it carted away. And I can't bring myself to trash it. It doesn't do any harm here, and I don't need the space."

She walked to the piano and ran her fingers down the keys from top to bottom. "It could use tuning," she noted.

"So could we all," he replied.

"But it's still playable. The temperature and humidity up here must be good for it. This looks like a great house for pianos and people."

"So where do you live now?"

"On a friend's couch."

"No wonder this place looks good to you, even in its present condition."

"Before that, I lived with Jack, my ex-boyfriend, in a big old house in Newton. He was like a visitor in his own house. A cleaning service cleaned the place. A yard service took care of the lawn. He could have moved out at any time with no regrets. He wasn't committed to it."

"Check the view from over here," Tom suggested. She thought he was embarrassed by the direction of the conversation, then realized that, no, he sensed that she was saying more than she wanted to, and he wanted to spare her awkwardness. "If you like, we could step through the open window and go out on the walkway."

"Walkway?"

"There's a path around the outside of the attic next to the castle-like rampart. People who don't mind heights love it. Myself, I prefer to enjoy the view behind windows and walls."

"Walls are good," she agreed with a smile, relieved at the return to impersonal chatter.

Then she looked up and exclaimed, "A cupola. I was in such a hurry to see the inside, I didn't take a good look at the outside of this building. The house I grew up in had a cupola. I used to think of it as a leprechaun hut perched on top of our house. The view must be amazing."

He set the ladder in place and led the way. The only furniture up there was a folded chair. There was just enough room for the two of them to stand without touching.

She felt awkward being so close to him. She stared out the window at the roofs of other Victorian buildings along Fairfield Street.

"You must love it up here."

"I do now. These last few months I've been coming here often to read or just to think."

"And before?"

"I was wrapped up in my work, getting home late, and at home continuing to work on my projects. I took great pride in my work. I wasn't around for Diane when she needed me. She became independent out of necessity. When the kids left the nest, she left, too. And no sooner did she walk out, than my job was exported to India, and I had all this downtime—time that I could have enjoyed with her, if she were still here..."

"How long have you lived here?"

"All my life."

"So your parents ...?"

"Yes, my father was born here, and his father. My great-grandfather bought the place when it was new. That's not a brag," he quickly added. "They weren't wealthy. Just ordinary people with a house to hand down to their kids. And the kids liked it here and saw no reason to move."

"And your kids?"

"Laurel is married now and living in Asheville, North Carolina. And Mark moved out as soon as he was old enough to."

"In the divorce, your ex wanted to sell it, didn't she?"

"Yes, but we compromised. She has our summer place at the Cape, in Chatham. That's where she lives now. She added heat and had it insulated and bought a dog. She likes taking long walks on the beach."

"So, if you own the whole building, why do you have to rent a room in your own apartment? This building ought to be worth two or three million, and those three other apartments must each bring in at least $2,500 a month."

"$3,000."

"So why do you want to rent a room?"

"When I was negotiating the divorce, I had a good job. My one concern was keeping the house. So, I made a deal—Diane could have the place at the Cape and monthly alimony payments equal to what we were getting in rent for those three apartments below us. As it turned out, I lost my job just a few days after the divorce became final. And I haven't found a new job yet, just some freelance work now and then. So, my financial situation is not at all what I expected. I have to rent this room to make ends meet."

"Yes," she muttered.

"What?" he asked

"Yes," she said again, louder. Then she realized what she had said and regretted she had said it so quickly. She needed to think rationally. There were too many complications.

"You mean you'll take me; I mean the room?" he beamed with delight.

She looked away. He was too happy. She felt too good. It was all wrong. If this was to work, there had to be limits, and he had to understand there were limits. Silently, she looked out over the city. She sensed him close behind her, tense, waiting for her to say more, to firmly close the deal.

A sparrow hawk, soared past the window and up the street, catching an updraft toward the Prudential Tower. She followed its flight until it was out of sight.

Then she saw two people—a man and a woman—approaching the building with speed and determination, from different directions. That broke her reverie. This opportunity wouldn't last forever.

She turned and looked him in the eye, "I need to juggle money from one bank account to another, to pay the first month's rent and a security deposit." The words came out quickly, as if she had rehearsed them. But she didn't really know what she was going to say until she said it. "I hadn't expected to find a place so soon—this is my first day of house hunting. There's a branch of my bank nearby. I can run and be back in less than an hour. Please hold it for me."

"Hold it? No problem. It isn't like hundreds of people are pounding on the door."

"But they will be soon."

"What?"

"Down there," she pointed. "I see two coming now..."

Approaching from the left, a young man was staring intently at a device in his hand, probably with GPS, guiding him to this building.

And a very young blond woman was approaching from the right.

"Well, the room is taken. It's yours. Period," he said.

As she followed him down the ladder to the attic and down the next ladder to the apartment and through the apartment to the stairs, she noticed the kitchen phone was off the hook. No wonder he hadn't gotten any other answers to his ad. She reached out to hang it up, then stopped herself—first she should make sure the deal was firm.

3 ~ The Family Assembles

Patti had just arrived by bus from Plymouth, NH. She had no luggage.

After a summer trekking through Europe with friends, she had returned home to pack and leave for the University of Michigan in Ann Arbor, only to find a letter from Boston University telling her that she had been accepted off the waiting list. With just a week left before school was to start, she caught the first bus to Boston to find a place to live.

BU had been her first choice, not so much for the school as for the city—the Red Sox, the Patriots, the Celtics, Ally McBeall, Cheers, the river, the shops. The first time her parents had taken her to Boston was for a Red Sox victory parade through the city—her city now, if she could just find a room to rent.

Checking the online ads on her iPhone, she only found one listing within walking distance of campus—a room on the fourth floor of a building between BU and Copley Square. Calling in the early morning, as soon as she spotted the ad, the phone went straight to voicemail. Probably busy. Plenty of people would want a room at such an ideal location.

She wished she had the full address. She'd keep calling. She had already added the number to her speed dial. Meanwhile, she had better check the BU housing office in case they had listings.

From South Station, she took the Red Line to Downtown Crossing, then the Orange Line to Back Bay, then walked to Boylston Street and caught the Green Line outbound. Awkward and around about. She'd know better next time.

Her mind wandered, imagining what it would be like to be a freshman in Boston. Then she realized half a dozen guys were staring at her. She avoided eye contact. She had gotten used to dressing this way over the last couple of months, mimicking the style of others her age who she saw at youth hostels in France and Italy. Jeans worn low, with the straps of her panties showing. That look felt natural to her now. But from the reactions of those guys, this was not the way to dress in Boston.

Growing up, she had moved a lot as her parents divorced and remarried, then divorced again. But she had always lived in the same region, and always in small towns. It might take a while to adjust to city living.

The subway stopped with a jolt. She jumped up and rushed out, afraid to miss her station; only to discover that this was Hynes Center, one stop short of Kenmore Square, where she had wanted to go.

She took another look at her map of downtown Boston. Kenmore Square was maybe four blocks away. It was a beautiful day. She could walk it, rather than take the next train.

She headed down Massachusetts Avenue to Newbury Street, then, in no hurry, back-tracked down Newbury, checking the shops.

Then she turned left at Fairfield, heading toward Commonwealth, where she planned to take another left and walk straight to BU.

Ahead, she spotted an attractive young man racing toward her.

He halted two steps in front of her.

She stopped and smiled at him, inviting eye contact.

He was staring at his cell phone, a GPS map on the screen. He didn't notice her. Rather, he turned toward the building beside them and raced up the stairs.

She then spotted the sign in the window of the building—"Room for Rent". She opened her iPhone and went to the listing she had bookmarked—"Downtown Boston, between BU and Copley Square, Fairfield Street, fourth floor".

Then she raced after him, shouting, "Hey. What are you doing? I saw that first."

He ignored her. He buttoned his top shirt button, pushed back his unkempt hair, and rang the doorbell.

Patti stood beside him, fuming, as they waited at the door.

***

When Tom opened the front door of the building to let Marge out, he found himself face-to-face with the woman and the man they had seen from the cupola. Tom was on an emotional high from meeting Marge. His mind was racing ahead, making a to-do list—what to straighten, what furniture to buy, how to handle food-shopping and meals. He wasn't in the mood to deal with other prospective renters.

"I'm sorry, but the room is taken," he announced gruffly.

"Fourth floor, right?" asked the young man.

"Yes."

"Great location. I'd like to take a look."

Before Tom could reply, the young man raced up the stairs, and the girl, too, squeezed past him.

"Thank you," she whispered, with a wide smile, on the way by.

Tom stared after them in disbelief.

"Aren't you going to stop them?" Marge asked sharply.

"The room is yours, period," he replied.

"Well, that's great. But you left your apartment door open, and two total strangers are headed there now."

Jolted back to reality, Tom ran up the stairs. Marge followed him.

They caught up with the girl and the young man in the kitchen/dining room, where the girl was looking out the window and the young man was looking at the stack of mail on the kitchen table.

Tom growled, "Who the hell are you?

"Alex O'Reilly, pleased to meet you, Tom."

"How did you know my name?"

"It was in your ad, and it's all over your mail."

Tom was speechless.

The girl pointed at the Free Cell game on the screen of the laptop and asked, "Are you done here?"

"Yes," Tom admitted, "completely dead-ended."

"Well, not completely." She sat down and in a few quick moves won the game.

Tom stared and muttered, "And who are you?"

"Cleopatra de Navarre. Patti for short."

Tom's eyes followed her as she got up, walked over to the refrigerator, and glanced at the tattered kids' drawings attached to the door with magnets.

He couldn't help but stare at her—the short top, the bra straps pulled to the side so they would show, the bare midriff, the jeans way low on her hips, the straps of her blue bikini panties pulled high so they'd show, too. Thank God his daughter had grown up before the advent of this provocative style. He could imagine that Patti's parents rarely got a good night's sleep. But here she was alone in the city. She didn't seem to know Alex. What parents would let a girl like this shop alone for a place to live?

"May I peek inside?" she asked politely, with her hand on the refrigerator.

"Sure," Tom replied, without thinking.

The freezer was full of TV dinners, and the refrigerator was full of Coke cans.

"May I have a Coke?" she asked sweetly.

"Sure, help yourself." He would have found it difficult to say no to anything she might request.

She took one and started sipping, very much at home.

Then Tom remembered Marge, who was leaning against the kitchen counter by the sink. She looked far less self-assured than she had a few minutes before. Tom realized that he was smiling broadly at the new girl with the bare midriff—this girl who was younger than his daughter. He was tempted to reassure Marge that the room was hers, to eliminate any uncertainty—she deserved that from him. She had so readily agreed to move in, despite his scruffy appearance and the embarrassing disorder of the apartment. But he hesitated, not because he might change his mind, but rather because this was the first time he had seen Marge with her defenses down, vulnerable.

Breaking the silence, Marge announced to the newcomers, "My name is Margaret Manchester; and I just rented the room."

"Patti here."

"And I'm Alex, Alex O'Reilly."

They both ignored her comment about the rental. Alex wandered into the living room, while Patti headed for the bedrooms.

"Are you just going to sit there while they—"

"Relax, Marge. They're good kids."

"'Good kids'? You don't know anything about them."

"My instinct says..."

"What instinct?"

"The same instinct that told me that you are the one."

Marge was so wound up that she didn't register what he had said. "I bet she's a runaway, and, for all you know, he could be a burglar casing the place."

Tom countered, "My gut tells me to trust them, to let them poke around a bit. Imagine they were your kids—would you want them to be rejected out-of-hand?"

"If Patti were my daughter," she insisted, "I'd have never let her go house-hunting alone. This is a city. She should know the risks, the kooky people she could hook up with. So she's either a runaway, or her parents are totally irresponsible. Either way she's trouble waiting to happen."

Tom chuckled. "I'd figure Alex for twenty, and Patti for eighteen—a couple of college kids."

"I'd peg her as a sixteen-year-old runaway, too mature and experienced for her age."

"Okay, she's blond. I get it. But what about Alex? What do you have against him?"

"The jeans with holes worn in the knees, the open flannel shirt worn on top of a Beatles tee-shirt? That's too 'Joe College' to be 'Joe College'. He's a ne'er-do-well imitating the look. I bet he's not in school and doesn't have a job and wouldn't be able to pay his rent. I don't trust him."

"Wow! You don't pull punches, do you? And what do you think of me?"

She flinched, then stared blankly. Finally, she was able to mumble, "What did you say?"

"What do you think of me?"

"No, before that."

"Let's see—rewind tape." He put his hand on his forehead as he tried to remember. "Maybe, the line about instinct, that my instinct told me that you are the one."

"Yes, that's the line. And, yes, your instincts are right on target," she relaxed and smiled. "Let them look till the kangaroos come home. May I have a Coke?"

"Sure, help yourself."

She took a Coke from the refrigerator, then sat down at the table, across from Tom and sipped and watched as he surfed the Web and basked in her attention.

***

Patti opened the door to the master bedroom and shut it; then opened the door to another bedroom, and walked in. The only furniture was an end table and a rocking chair. A box of stuffed animals lay near the door to the kitchen.

She walked straight to the end table and picked up a framed photo of a young woman wearing a graduation cap and gown. She turned toward a mirror on the wall and held the picture up next to her face, to confirm that there was a resemblance, though the girl in the photo had brown hair.

Then she explored the box, pulling out Cabbage Patch Kids and Pooh characters, and arranging them along the floor by the wall. Then she lay down on the floor, resting her head on a stack of Puffalumps, with a faraway look, remembering.

Alex entered the room through the door from the office.

"Making yourself at home?" he asked.

"I've had so many homes, I don't know which one I belong in," she explained. "I was born into a *Donna Reed* and *Father Knows Best* kind of world. That blew up. Then the pieces blew up. More marriages, more divorces. It takes me an entire address book just to list the members of my step-families."

"I'm a loner," volunteered Alex, distracted, looking at the wall above Patti's head. "Only child of absentee parents. But I have connections."

"Business connections?" she asked, puzzled that he still paid no attention to her looks. No male near her age had ever ignored her physical presence like this.

"Of course."

"Well, please make the best of those connections of yours and find another place. I seriously need this one. I got into BU from the waiting list—a total miracle. But now school starts in a week, and there isn't a room to be had in all of Boston."

"Except this one."

"Yes, this would be perfect for me. You can wait. You can find something else. To you, there's nothing special about this place."

"Are you kidding? It sits dead center on a wireless Internet hot spot—a great location from which to run a global business."

"Like you could run a business..."

"From a hot spot like this—with both high speed access and anonymity—I could perform miracles."

"So you won't help me? You won't back down? You really won't let me have this place?"

"I'm not the one you've got to convince." He opened the door to the kitchen enough so the two of them could hear Tom and Marge

***

"How many ways do I have to say it? The room is yours," Tom emphasized.

"But, seriously, you don't know anything about me."

"I like what I see and what I know."

"I'm a psychologist, a social psychologist, working on government research grants."

"And that matters because ...?"

"Because you can count on me to pay the rent."

"I never doubted that."

"You're too trusting. You should ask for references."

"Do you have references?"

"I can give you my boss and my boss's boss. But I don't have any housing-related references."

Tom smiled. "Okay, I won't call your ex-boyfriend, if you don't call my ex-wife."

"Your openness is disarming."

"We complement one another."

"Is that an insult?"

"Only if you want to take it that way."

"You're too agreeable."

"Only if you want me to be."

"You're desperate."

"That, too."

"I really don't know anything about you."

"Forty-five. Unemployed computer programmer. Twenty-five years at the same job. The company kept changing ownership, but I stayed put until they decided to pay somebody in India half as much to do the same work."

"So you're depressed. Low self-esteem. That's probably more than I can handle right now."

"So I'm down on my luck. But I've got a good track record, and I'm going to make a comeback.

"And the kids?"

"They're far away—North Carolina and California."

"Yes, you told me about Laurel and Mark. I mean the kids who are casing out your apartment, the ones listening to us from the bedroom over there. Are they in the running?"

"It's yours. Period."

"Wait," shouted Patti and Alex.

***

All four of them assembled at the make-shift kitchen table, Tom and Marge on folding card-table chairs, Patti on a beanbag she brought in from the living room, and Alex on a desk chair he brought from the office.

Marge sat up straight with her arms crossed, elbows tight to her sides. She was guardedly optimistic. She had committed to take the room, and rationally she was pleased with that outcome. But at the same time, she dreaded what might come from such an unorthodox living situation. If they could find space for one more roomer, that might relieve the tension. But, at first glance, these two did not look like good candidates. Alex struck her as devious and secretive; and Patti as devious and gregarious. She wasn't sure which would be worse. She could imagine Patti's friends hanging out here, making noise into the night.

"So you were listening?" Marge asked them, her tone accusatory. "Okay, Patti and Alex, let's get down to business."

Patti turned toward Tom, who, leaning back like a spectator, seemed more flexible than Marge. Patti handed him the photo of his daughter that she had found in her inspection of the apartment.

"Yes," Tom admitted, "the resemblance is amazing. But I'm not in the market for a new daughter. I'm just looking for rent."

"And someone compatible to live with," Alex prompted him. "Someone with knowledge and skills and connections that could help you."

"And I'm sure you would like to help someone who really needs help, Tom," Patti countered. "Like a college freshman, who needs a place to live, or she won't be able to start school next week. Like someone from out-of-town, who could benefit from your wisdom and experience."

Tom interpreted, "You mean a teenage daughter who not only listens, but even asks for advice? I thought that species was extinct."

"I think we've had enough of this," Marge took charge again. "Tom, you said the room is mine. I told you I want it. Sorry, kids, but you're wasting your time."

Tom hesitated, "But there's something about these two. And the apartment has felt so empty since my kids moved out. Maybe by shifting things around, we could take on a second roomer."

"God," exclaimed Marge. "Of course you'd be better off with a second rent, and another person might help in other ways—but we'd want someone mature and independent, with a steady income. Either of these kids would mean trouble."

"Hey, don't sweat it," suggested Tom. "This shouldn't take long. And you can do the interviewing. After all, you're a professional interviewer, right?"

Marge took a deep breath, paused to gather her thoughts, then addressed Patti and Alex, in a cold impartial voice, "So you've seen the place, and you both like it, And I'm sure there are hundreds of others who would be here already if the phone weren't off the hook."

"The phone is off the hook?" asked Tom.

He started to head toward the phone, but Marge intercepted. "Tom, there's no need for that. Things are complicated enough already. We have to sort this out calmly, without the phone ringing, without your listening to hundreds of messages." Then feeling a twinge of guilt, she added, "But these two showed initiative, finding this place quickly without a specific address. It's only fair to give them a hearing. And if you were willing to sacrifice, maybe giving up your office, you probably could take on a second roomer."

She turned to Patti, "So in thirty words or less, who are you and what are you doing here? Why are you looking for a place to live in Boston?"

"I'm eighteen. I'll be a freshman. I got into BU way late, after the on-campus housing was gone."

"And how did you end up house hunting alone?"

"I spent the summer trekking around Europe with friends. When I got home, I found the letter from BU saying I was accepted from the waiting list. So I called BU to tell them that I was coming, and the next morning I caught the first bus to Boston. I left my parents a note. They'll understand."

"So where are these oh-so-understanding parents?"

"George and Mary are probably at our place on Squam Lake with their cell phones turned off."

"George and Mary? Why not Mom and Dad?"

"Well, Dad's in Vermont. And Mom's in LA, I think."

"What?"

"After Dad and Mom split, I went with him. Mary is Dad's second wife. Then Mary and Dad split, and I went with her, and she married George. And Mom and Dad have both remarried. Some people find that a bit confusing, but when you grow up like that, and it's the only kind of family you've ever known, it feels natural. And George and Mary are great. I could never hope for better parents."

"God," exclaimed Marge. "And you, Alex, what do you do?"

"This and that."

"Oh, yes, This and That, Incorporated. I hear they pay well and have great benefits."

"I like your wit. You come on a bit strong, but you're fast and sharp. You get right to the point. If I were shopping for a Mom, you'd be the one."

"Thank you, I think. But my guess is that you don't go to school, and you don't have a regular job."

"It's more complicated than that. I have business connections," Alex insisted, his eyes not making contact with hers.

"I'm sure you do," Marge continued. "You probably have great fun emailing your friends and brainstorming about Internet startup ideas. But how would you pay the rent?"

"Money isn't a problem. Honest. I could pay six months in advance, in cash."

"Now that sounds interesting," noted Tom.

"Too interesting," countered Marge. "Are you gambling or dealing drugs?"

Alex laughed. "What an imagination you have' I love it."

"Well, however you came by that money, it won't last forever. At your age—"

"Twenty."

"Yes, at twenty, you need to get yourself in gear, do things that will move you forward, prepare for a real career, a real life, for God's sake."

"I'm quite happy, thank you."

"That's the problem. You're too complacent, too content to do nothing. And you probably have no marketable skills. Just having a wad of money in your pocket doesn't make you a respectable citizen and a desirable apartment-mate. Why should Tom pick you?"

Rather than answer, he took hold of Tom's laptop.

"What are you doing with my computer?"

"This apartment is on a WiFi hotspot," Alex explained. "That means you can have high-speed wireless Internet for free. I could install a wireless modem and have you set up in a couple minutes."

Tom grinned and saluted, "Go for it."

Alex pulled a modem card and a software CD from his pocket and got to work.

Marge warned Tom, "Watch out. I don't trust that kid." She stood up suddenly and nearly lost her balance, tripping on a Coke can.

Patti laughed good-naturedly, "Well, at least they aren't beer cans."

"And no sign of smoking," Marge replied. "That's two points in his favor."

"I admit this place does need a woman's touch," Tom agreed, delighted at the attention he was getting.

"Or any touch at all," said Marge, checking the top of the refrigerator for dust.

As soon as Alex finished with the laptop, he got up to make way for Tom, who then sat down and started web surfing, delighted at the speed of response at his favorite sites.

"Patti," Marge concluded, "from the look on Tom's face, I'm afraid you're going to have to look for another room."

"Not so quick," suggested Tom, "Maybe we could make room for both of them."

Marge objected, "And who would double up?"

"No one," explained Tom. "The living room. We could partition it off with a sliding door and make that into another bedroom. I rent two of my apartments to groups of students; and in both cases they've done the same thing."

"But what about our stuff?" asked Patti. "With four people here, would there be any room for storage?"

Marge hesitated, then realized that the situation would be far less awkward with all of them living here—two women and two men, from two different generations. "The attic," she said out loud.

"This place has an attic?" asked Alex.

"A huge attic," Marge explained, suddenly anxious to make this work. "It's unfinished, probably haunted, and no good for living space but great for storage."

Patti interjected, "Life is like an attic."

"What does that mean?" asked Tom.

Patti replied, "The word 'attic' just triggered an old memory. My dad, George, says that often."

"But what does it mean?" asked Tom.

"I don't know," Patti admitted. "I always tuned him out."

"Sometimes life is like an attic," Marge echoed, and then continued, "What you want and need is right there if you could just find it."

They agreed that Marge would take the old master bedroom; Patti would take Laurel's old room. Tom would move into what was then his office. Alex, who admitted he had claustrophobic tendencies, would take the living room, which was larger than the others, although it wouldn't have the same degree of quiet and privacy, even after they partitioned it off from the kitchen with a sliding door.

The kitchen would serve as their social center.

They could share the storage space in the attic. "It's like in one of those house make-over shows," Patti noted. "In a day or two, we could make this place just the way we want it."

"Yes," Tom agreed. "Working together on this project we can get to know one another and learn to adjust to one another's needs. And my getting three rents instead of one could solve a lot of problems."

"Three rents?" Marge questioned immediately. "You expect us to each pay what you were asking for in the first place? We're to do the work of turning this mess into livable space? We're to put up with the crowding? And you want us all to pay full price?"

"Well, maybe not full. We could talk about that later."

"Now," Marge insisted.

"Three-quarters each," Tom suggested.

"Two-thirds," Alex countered. "That way you end up with two full rents."

"Deal," Tom agreed.

"Provided you pay for the furniture," Marge added.

"Mattresses on the floor can be surprisingly comfortable," Tom suggested.

Marge and Patti glared at him. Alex just laughed.

"Okay, okay," Tom relented. "I'll buy some beds."

"And we need a real kitchen table, too," insisted Marge.

"And paint," Patti added. "All these rooms could use a fresh coat of paint."

"And rugs and curtains," Marge remembered.

"Okay, okay. I surrender. Just nothing extravagant."

Marge left to buy cleaning supplies and equipment. Patti made a shopping list of furniture, curtains, and paint. Tom and Alex moved the big-screen TV from the living room to the kitchen.

After two days of work getting the apartment into shape, Tom took a break in the attic, sitting in a stuffed chair among the old toys and memorabilia of his kids, trying to absorb what had just happened, how rapidly his life had changed—it felt so good. It felt too good. He wished he had someone to confide in, to sort through it all; someone he could trust to validate his judgement—someone like his ex. No, not Diane. This was a turning point, a new beginning, and a good one—he was sure, almost sure.

That was when Tom went to Flanagan's and saw the British tourist hit by the cab, and Tracy asked him about the room, and he talked too much to the stranger in the Red Sox hat.

4 ~ First Night

After the accident, Tom avoided Flanagan's for three nights, then ducked back in, just after supper and sat in a dark corner. Tracy spotted him. He cringed as she approached.

"It's taken," she said.

"The table?"

"No, the room—your room."

"Yeah," he mumbled into his beer, avoiding those penetrating blue eyes.

"I found out the next day. You must have been uncomfortable, me asking like that."

"Yeah. I was kicking myself."

"It's okay. I found another place. Not far off. Some student got into another college off the waiting list and did a quick shift."

"Good," he replied half-heartedly. "So who told you it was taken?"

"That guy you were with the night of the accident."

"The one in the Red Sox hat?"

"That's the one. He came back the next night asking for you."

When business slowed down, near closing time, Tracy joined him in his dark corner.

"I feel I know you well already," she told him. "Bill says you asked about me, repeatedly. He says the more you heard the more you wanted to know. Then your reaction to the woman in the accident was so earnest, responsible. And when I asked you about the room for rent, you should have seen your face. You were tempted, but you held back. You stayed loyal to your new tenants. You did what you thought was right, though you were conflicted about it. And that guy in the Red Sox hat told me about that fantasy of yours."

"What fantasy?"

"Staying up all night with a woman you care for—talking non-stop and doing nothing but talk. What a turn on."

Tom cringed to hear his words misconstrued that way. When he talked to that stranger in the Red Sox hat, he had been fishing for a metaphor to explain the effect that Marge had on him. He should never have talked so loosely to a stranger.

Tracy continued, "You realize, of course, that if I'd rented that room from you, I couldn't have gone out with you. It would have been too awkward. But now that won't be a problem, will it?"

When Flanagan's closed, Tom walked with Tracy back to her apartment. It was five stories up, on the top floor of a building like Tom's. What had been the attic had been converted into five studio apartments, separated by thin plasterboard partitions. It was 1 a.m., but they were bombarded by sound from all sides—hip hop, classic rock, a TV show with canned laughter, and heavy panting that may or may not have been on television.

Tom, distracted by the noise, was lost in her blue eyes and exhilarated by her attention. He was uncertain what she might expect next and how he might perform, if it came to that. He talked non-stop, and she listened patiently, holding his hand, stroking the middle of his back, and their eyes locked.

He explained about the stiff leg. When he was ten, big for his age, athletic, with dreams of sports prowess in high school and college, he broke his left leg in a pick-up football game. While home from school and healing, he read *Treasure Island* for the first time. For years after that, his favorite make-believe game was Treasure Attic; he was Long John Silver, and the attic of their house in Back Bay, with its old trunks and boxes, was the hiding place for pirate treasure.

The following spring, in the local Little League playoffs, he slugged what should have been the game-winning hit. When he was racing from third base to home, his left leg went stiff. He tripped, then crawled, and was tagged out. His team lost.

A few weeks later, a bully at school mocked him, imitating the incident. Tom raced at him, his leg working just fine. Then suddenly, the leg went stiff again. The bully doubled over with laughter. Tom hit him with an upper cut, then kicked high and hard with that stiff left leg. After that, no one at school dared to mock him to his face again.

He was in college when the Disney movie of *Treasure Island*, with Robert Newton as Long John Silver, came out on videotape. Tom watched it over and over, even when he was supposed to be studying for exams. He and Diane, his wife-to-be, had fun with pirate-and-damsel role-play in the attic.

When he proposed to Diane, his leg went stiff again. He couldn't kneel, and he doubled over laughing like the bully had so long before, imagining how silly he looked. Diane laughed, too, and said she would be his pirate queen. Later she admitted to him that she had planned to say "no" if he ever proposed. She thought theirs was just a fling, and they would move on after college. But seeing him like that—so stressed that the old trigger went off—she realized that she loved him. not the everyday nice guy, but rather the kid he was inside, the kid who got strength from pretending he was a peg-legged pirate. She found that bizarre mixture of vulnerability and strength endearing, that when faced with a crisis, he went lame, and the lameness put him back in touch with his real self and gave him the strength that he needed.

Then he chuckled as he remembered, "Long John Silver didn't have a peg leg. He was missing a leg. It was cut off close to the hip, and he had a crutch under his left shoulder. When he couldn't get hold of the crutch, he had to hop to get around. I confused him with Captain Ahab from *Moby Dick*, who had an artificial leg made of whalebone."

"No matter," insisted Tracy. "It's the perception, not the reality that counts. The connection between your broken leg and Silver's missing leg was in the back of your mind. It's still there, as we saw the night of the accident."

"Okay, Detective Tracy." Unlike Diane, she seemed attracted by a tough-guy image of him. "So you like thinking of me as a modern-day Long John Silver?"

"Let's see. He was a cook, who was handy with a sword and a flint-lock pistol."

"And he could also throw his crutch like a spear."

"A useful skill in the twenty-first century," she noted.

"So what tough-guy skills do you think I should have?" he played along.

"Think Humphrey Bogart as Sam Spade. Think Robert Parker's Spenser."

"That's not me."

"That's what this is about, isn't it? You aren't happy about who you are. 'Midway on the journey of our life ....' The whole Dante bit."

"What are you getting at?"

"Your life. It's half over. Probably more than half."

"Half full, I prefer to think."

"Well, there's another side of you that thinks empty, that feels empty. It's like you haven't started your real life yet."

"That's not me. I don't worry much about tomorrow. When Diane would heckle me about planning ahead, I'd just say, 'We'll cross that finger when we come to it. We'll burn that bridge when we come to it.'"

"Well, who do you think you are?"

"I'm a middle-aged, divorced, unemployed software engineer. Have I eaten enough humble pie? Are you satisfied now?"

"And if your life were a novel, would you want that guy to be the hero of the story?"

"My life isn't a novel."

"Everyone's life is. But not many of them are worth reading."

"Or living."

"You said it."

"So are you going to be my editor?"

"Rewrite yourself, and I'll be happy to kibitz. But you have to get started on your own."

"So I should take writing classes?"

"Engage gears. Get out of neutral. Connect with the people around you. Don't just watch—do."

"Do what?"

"Whatever you'd regret not doing."

"You're a control freak," he told her.

"Are you putting me down?"

"I'd rather pick you up."

"I don't know what to make of you."

"But you already said it—I'm a naive innocent middle-aged man who needs to start living."

"And what do you think of me?"

"You're so sexy you could turn on anyone. You could turn on a dime."

That night they acted out the fantasy that Tom had mentioned to the stranger—they talked until dawn, cuddling and hugging.

5 ~ Attic Attack

Tom didn't know what to expect next. The all-night no-sex talkathon had taken him into new territory with Tracy.

Diane had been passive, taking her cues from him. In life as on the dance floor, he was expected to lead, to drive, to decide, until at the end, she resented that he had ignored her needs and taken her for granted and not heeded what to her had been clear signals.

And here was Tracy—aggressive, self-assured, taking charge. He didn't know what to expect from her next, but the surprise was part of the thrill and the pleasure.

As a kid he never enjoyed roller coasters. Now he would probably love such a ride with Tracy beside him.

Ironically, Tracy's strong-willed manner brought out aspects of Tom that he had never suspected, and hence gave him a sense of his potential for change, at a time in life when he might have settled for being who he thought he was for the rest of his days.

And who was she? Every inch of wall space in her studio apartment was taken up with bookcases. But the shelves were empty. She had explained that when her divorce was final, she wanted to make a fresh start in a place where she had never been before, and to take charge of her life. Maybe she was over-compensating, and the real Tracy, who he had not yet seen, had a very different personality. Or maybe she had grown and changed into someone very different from the person she had been before.

She explained that she arrived in Boston with no baggage—literally. She had money from savings and from the divorce settlement, and she had decided to leave behind all the things that had been part of her previous life.

She intended to buy a new library—hence the bookshelves. But when she connected to Amazon to buy the books, she saw the promos for their Kindle book reader, and she couldn't resist. Not only would she have a new library; she'd have a new way of owning and reading books—electronically. She explained that this little gadget, about the size of a paperback book, had a thousand books on it already, and she added two or three more each day, buying them over the Internet, using the Kindle's wireless connection.

On the desk by the one window, sat a laptop which she used to surf the Web and watch DVDs, and next to it sat her wallet and her Kindle. The bed was in the middle of the floor. Aside from the empty bookshelves, there was a closet-sized bathroom, and small kitchen area with a sink, a microwave, and a refrigerator. No bureau. She used the kitchen cabinets to store clothes. There were no pictures, no knick-knacks—nothing that could be interpreted as a tangible expression of her personality.

***

The building was quiet the second time they went up the stairs to Tracy's apartment. When they reached her landing, she turned off the hall light before opening her door. When he reached for the light switch inside, she pushed his hand aside, shut the door loudly, shoved him down on the bed and climbed on top of him in the dark.

No foreplay. Right there. Right then.

He heard a slight ripping sound, then felt her sliding a condom on him. She was on top. He remembered a scene with Gwyneth Paltrow in *Shakespeare in Love*.

Diane had never wanted to be on top. She preferred missionary. Passive, with lots of foreplay and a light on.

Making love in the dark was a new experience for him—sensuous and earthy and forbidden. It was like he had been living confined in a box before, and now the walls weren't there. Anything was possible. He felt like a teenager having sex for the first time. At that moment, Tracy wasn't a particular individual to him. She was every woman he had ever wanted.

Now and then lights from a passing car would flash through the window, bouncing off the ceiling and walls, backlighting her, like a full-body halo.

Then she was pressing and thrusting frantically. She, too, was caught up in the sensations. She wanted to use him as he wanted to use her. She wanted to come. She needed to come. He needed to stay hard long enough for her to finish. He tried not to think of her, tried to blank out these sensations or he would release completely at the next thrust. He forced himself to think of the Red Sox and the pitching match-ups for the upcoming series with the Yankees. And it worked. He stayed hard. She came.

And as she paused in ecstasy, the light of a passing car flashed again.

That's when he came, but not from a flood of pleasure that he could no longer postpone, but rather from fear at the shadow projected on the ceiling and walls.

A sharp crack and the sound of pieces of glass hitting the desk and floor.

The window opened, wood scraping loudly on wood.

A bright light flashed on.

Tom and Tracy, naked, clutched each other.

The light went out.

A loud rattle.

Sneakers moving fast over roof tiles, fading in the distance.

Tracy was the first to get up, put on a robe, turn on the light, shut the window, and call 911.

"He took my Kindle," she mumbled.

"What?"

"He left my wallet and the laptop on the desk. The only thing he took was my Kindle."

The police came about an hour after the call.

The burglar had left behind his flashlight. But the police didn't bother to take it with them. Little was missing. The incident wasn't worth investigating. The perp would have worn gloves to avoid leaving fingerprints. He was long gone. The cops just wanted to take care of the paperwork and move on to the next reported burglary.

The only times Tom had talked to cops before was to ask for directions, or to respond to their questions when they had pulled him over for minor traffic violations.

One cop did the writing, the other the talking.

Tom was disoriented. There was a lesson here, but he wasn't sure what it was. He felt helpless, unprepared, without a clue of what he should have done when the guy came through the window, or what he should do now.

The cop who was talking reassured him. "I don't think you were in any danger. You probably scared the hell out of the guy. In the rest of the buildings around here, this floor level is attic storage. He probably had a shopping list of stuff his fence wanted. He didn't expect to find people here. He's probably still running. It may be days before he builds up enough gumption to do this again."

Tom tried to think like a detective would think, "You see the small hole in the windowpane right over the latch? That's just like the break-in in my attic."

"And you live where?"

"Just a few blocks from here, on Fairfield Street."

"And when was this break-in of yours?"

"I discovered the damage just a few days ago, but I can't say when it happened. Maybe months ago, maybe more. I don't go up there often."

"And you filed a report?"

"No."

"Why?"

"Nothing important was taken—just some old plate silver that I never used."

"No floorboards torn up or walls bashed in?"

"No."

"Then I guess it wasn't the Treasure Attic burglar."

"The what?"

"Probably just another copycat."

"Treasure what?"

"I thought you were a computer guy."

"Yeah."

"But you don't read the blog?"

"What blog?"

"Some anonymous guy has been reporting on attic burglaries in the Back Bay."

"Are there lots of them?"

"Dozens. Drives us nuts. This blog guy makes it a lot worse. Romanticizing it all—speculating that there must be some hidden treasure the burglars are after."

"Weird. And scary. But I guess we can rest easy," Tom added. "Once this guy hits an attic, he probably moves on to the next and the next. He'd have no reason to return to a place he hit before. Right?"

"Wrong. It may have started out as one burglar, but thanks to our blogger friend, there might be half a dozen copycats doing the same on their own. And the one doesn't know where the others have hit. Besides the Treasure Attic thing may have them thinking the mother lode is near. Some places get hit again and again."

"Again?" asked Tracy. "There's no way you'd catch me sleeping in this place again, not until this thing blows over."

"And how long might that be?" Tom asked the cops.

"Weeks. Months. Years maybe. Thanks to the blogger."

"And you have no idea who he is?"

"The burglar?"

"The blogger."

"Tech's not my thing, but I hear he keeps changing his IP address and masking his identity. For all we know, he might be one of the burglars himself, muddying the water on purpose."

Tracy was too spooked to stay in her apartment; so Tom offered to take her to his place.

"Everybody's asleep by now. We can sleep until mid-afternoon when they'll all be gone," Tom explained. "Nobody need know that you were ever there."

"You mean I won't get to meet your roomers?"

"You can meet them later. After you've had a chance to put your life back together. We'll have you over for dinner—a sit-down dinner with the lot of them."

It was 4 a.m. when they walked through the door of his apartment.

"It's just the way I imagined it, said Tracy. "You described it so well."

"Hush," Tom whispered. "Everyone's asleep."

"So behind the sliding doors, that's what used to be the living room and is now a bedroom?" she whispered back.

"Yes, that's Alex's room. And the door over there near the refrigerator is to what used to be my master bedroom. Marge is there. And Patti's in the next room, which used to be my daughter's."

"And the door to your room, which used to be your son's room, then your office, is between the bathroom and Alex's."

"Yes," answered another whisper, as Alex came out of his room.

Tom took a deep, annoyed breath, "Alex, this is my friend Tracy."

Alex was in jeans, with a wide-open flannel shirt over a tee-shirt with blue wildflowers and the slogan "I have the right to live in my own reality".

"Is that slogan from the SyFy Channel?" Tracy asked softly.

"The quote? I don't know where it came from. I just like the expression."

Tom interrupted, testy, "This isn't the time or the place for conversation. It's four in the morning and people are asleep."

Tracy ignored Tom and answered Alex. "It probably resonates with how you see yourself."

"How do you figure that?"

"Tom says you're a loner, only child of absentee parents."

"Yeah, but I have connections—lots of connections."

"And that's a very memorable smile."

"Nice shoes," he noted, looking at her bare feet.

Tracy laughed, "We left in a hurry."

"Left where?"

"My place."

Tom interrupted, "A burglar broke into her attic apartment tonight."

"Attic?"

"Yes. Just a few blocks from here."

"What did he take?

"Only her Kindle."

"The cops?"

"They came, they saw, they yawned."

"Same old, same old?"

"Exactly."

Alex started typing rapidly on his laptop at the kitchen table. "Great stuff."

"What?"

"More fodder for my blog."

"You're the blogger?"

"You've heard of me?"

"One of the cops mentioned."

"A fan?"

"What's the opposite of a fan?"

"Well, a devoted reader."

"Yeah, that's it."

"That's what keeps a blogger going."

"And why do you do it?"

"Because the cops don't."

"And why should they?"

"Pull the community together. Get everybody to help fight crime and help the victims."

"I don't get it. How could a blog do that?"

"The details."

"What?"

"Like the Kindle. Not many people have those yet. Someone tries to fence one of those on the street, odds are that's hers."

"Wow," Tracy exclaimed, too loud, then covered her mouth as if that would lessen the noise.

"Power for the powerless," Alex went on.

"And the treasure hunt bit?"

"Just a theory of mine. Trying to make sense of the damage, the vandalism. I guess you two scared him away before that could happen."

"I guess so," Tracy whispered. "He turned on his flashlight, and instead of an attic full of collectibles, he saw Tom and me naked in bed."

"I can imagine. That must have interrupted your conversation."

Tracy chuckled, softly. "The guy's probably still running."

"You're not planning to go back there, are you?"

"Not tonight," Tom answered quickly.

"Well, don't mind me," said Alex, typing away. "I'll be busy for a while now."

Tom started toward his bedroom, but Tracy lingered and ventured, "You're the one who set up Tom on high-speed WiFi?"

"Yep. This building is on a great hotspot. That's how I found it."

"Okay, already," Tom interrupted, impatiently.

"Why, Tom," Tracy replied. "I detect a tone of jealousy. How sweet."

Tom cringed.

Tracy walked over to him, and wrapped her arms around his right arm, stroking his forearm sensuously with the tips of her fingers, and leaning toward his bedroom.

But Tom, still out of sorts, stayed put. "Alex, there's something more I wanted to tell you, that I should have told you before." "Yes?"

"Our building was broken into—before you moved in. I'm not sure when. In the attic. Someone broke the window just above the latch."

"Okay, another one to write about. Anything missing?"

"Just some old silver plate."

"Any vandalism?"

"No."

Alex nodded and continued typing.

"Aren't you upset that I didn't tell you before?"

"There are damned few buildings around here that haven't been hit yet."

"And that doesn't make you feel uncomfortable?"

"The burglar never goes downstairs to the residence."

"The cops think there are lots of them—copycats. They credit the blogger—you—for the popularity."

"I'm flattered."

6 ~ An Infestation of Burglars

In the luxurious restfulness between dream and waking, they cuddled, Tom and his bedmate spooned. Tom knew what he wanted. He knew who he was. Life was simple. Life was sweet.

But the mattress was on the floor. The walls were covered with his bookcases. The bedroom furniture was gone.

Diane was gone.

This wasn't Diane.

Her hand reached around and grasped his hardness and guided him into her from behind.

They moved together, blended together smoothly, naturally.

He came quickly, but remained firm enough, long enough for her to finish.

As she came, he whispered in her ear, "Marge."

The name sounded so strange and yet so right.

She turned and smiled at him—her bright blue eyes flashing. Tracy.

He quickly kissed her to mask his confusion. Had she heard? Had she understood? Or was she, like he, still half asleep?

She shut her eyes again and rolled back over, oh so comfortable, ready to return to sleep.

He caught sight of the clock on his desk—six o'clock. Still early. Too early to get up. He needed to get his bearings.

He heard the door to the apartment open. Voices. Patti back from school. Marge back from work. It was six in the evening. He was in bed with Tracy in his own apartment.

He quickly rolled off the mattress and pulled on his trousers and a tee-shirt.

Suddenly it was very important for him to explain, to cover up. He would act natural. He would say he had been job-hunting all day on the Web. He would offer to throw together supper. Tracy would sleep. Later, when the others were settled in their rooms, he would slip her out unnoticed. She would work her shift at Flanagan's. He would walk her back to her place.

He opened the door from his room to the kitchen and was about to spout the usual pleasantries, when Tracy, barefoot and wearing nothing but a tee-shirt of his, dashed by him and greeted a shocked Marge and Patti, like they were old friends.

Tom blurted out, "Remember, I told you about Tracy?"

"The waitress at Flanagan's?" asked Marge

"Yes."

"The one you stayed up with all night talking, just talking, when we were afraid you'd been mugged or hit by a car?" Marge pursued.

"Yes, I should have phoned."

"So you decided to continue your conversation here, so we wouldn't worry?"

"No. I mean that's not why."

"Why?"

"Her apartment was burglarized."

"And they took all her clothes? Poor thing."

"I mean a burglar broke in while she was there, while we were there."

"And interrupted your conversation? How horrid."

"You aren't making this easy."

Tracy, then Marge, then Patti all broke out laughing.

Alex popped in from his room. "This burglar bit is real."

"You can read all about it on his blog," Tracy added and laughed contagiously.

"Burglars have been hitting houses in the Back Bay," Alex explained. "They go from attic to attic, taking collectibles, sometimes tearing up the floorboards like they were looking for something."

"They hit here, too," Tom added quickly, relieved to divert the conversation away from Tracy's awkward presence.

"Burglars hit here tonight?" asked Marge.

"Not tonight," Alex answered, "but recently."

"Yes, recently," Tom affirmed.

"You mean that broken window?" "You noticed?"

"Of course I noticed. But I thought some kid threw a rock or something."

"Five stories up? Not likely," noted Alex.

"And right above the lock, and silver plate went missing," Tom added.

"So that's why you added the security service."

"Security service?"

"The labels on the attic windows."

"You noticed that too?"

"Of course. The next day after you showed me up there, you fixed the window and added those little warning labels."

"It would cost too much."

"What?"

"The service. I just stuck labels on the windows. I bought them on eBay a couple years ago. A friend told me about them. A modern-day equivalent of scarecrows."

Marge grabbed the pole, opened the trap door, and pulled down the ladder.

"What are you doing?"

"Checking to see if your scarecrows are working."

Tom grabbed the ladder and scampered up before Marge could.

The window at the top was intact. The other windows looked fine too. No sign of a further break-in. "All clear," he called.

Marge came up, checked the window and its lock, then strolled over to the piano and started playing the theme from the movie *The Sting*, with a honky-tonk rhythm.

Alex came next. He went straight to the window, unlatched it, opened it, and climbed out. He focused on details of the walkway and the ramparts, as if he were a professional looking for clues.

Then Tracy made her entrance, having quickly dressed for Flanagan's, with low-slung jeans and bare mid-riff, showing off her belly-button ring.

Tom wondered what Marge would look like dressed like that.

Then came Patti. She, too, had changed clothes. She was probably planning to go out with friends from school. But she still wore jeans low on her hips with the straps of her panties pulled high to show. To Tom, Tracy's look was risqué and enticing, but Patti's was embarrassing. Tracy, laughing, careered stiff-legged down the hallway and nearly collided with Patti. "Are these the famous crutches?" she asked.

"They probably are," Tom laughed. "I haven't seen those in over 30 years."

Tracy came to an awkward halt beside him, "Did you ever think of turning this attic into another apartment?"

"No. I'd need to build a staircase, bring up heat, add a bathroom, add a kitchen. I can't afford that kind of investment."

A knock on the wall. Another knock.

No one spoke. No one breathed.

Then a rhythmic shave-and-a haircut knocking.

"Is this place haunted?" asked Patti.

Tom stepped over to the wall and pounded the final "two bits" in reply. "He must have found it," Tom said. "Alex must have found it, with no hint to go by."

"Found what?" asked Marge.

"The hiding place."

"You mean there's a hidden room behind there?" asked Patti, with delight.

"Yes, indeed. A very special place."

"Like a place to hide runaway slaves, part of the Underground Railway?" she asked.

"No. In the days of the Underground Railway, the land this house sits on was under water. This house was built after the Back Bay was filled in, almost twenty years after the Civil War ended. And the hidden room was added to the original design by my Great-Grandpa Nat. He wanted his own private corner of the attic, where he could retreat and not be bothered by anybody. But Pru, my great-grandmother, laid claim to the entire attic, and Great-Granpa never got a chance to use it. Later, when Pru was too old to know or care, Dad used it. That's where he made ships in a bottle and read Gibbon's Rome."

"From your tone, I'd guess there's something special about that room—special for you," Marge noted.

"For me, it was a place to hide and be alone. It also has some romantic overtones, from college days, when I first dated Diane," he admitted. "To get there, you have to walk around the ramparts and climb in through the window."

Tracy and Patti climbed out the window and walked in the direction of the noise. Marge and Tom followed them slowly and cautiously, avoiding looking at the street five stories down.

"Holy Chicago," exclaimed Tracy. The window to the "secret" room was open and unbroken. That was the only way in, so it would never have been latched.

Alex stood in the middle of the room on a mattress with clean sheets, a pillow and a clean pillowcase.

On one side were three stacks of miscellaneous merchandise. On the other side were old trunks and boxes and an antique dress-maker's dummy that, from the dust, looked like they had been there for many decades.

"My God," exclaimed Marge. "The burglars are living here. They even dragged in a mattress."

"No," said Tom. "That's probably the same mattress Diane and I used."

"But not the freshly laundered sheets."

Patti attempted a lame joke, "At least our thief is tidy."

"Our thieves," Tracy corrected her.

"Definitely thieves," Alex affirmed.

Tom asked, "Have any of you heard noises up here at night?"

"Yeah," answered Patti. "I thought it was the pipes or something."

"But it's still warm outside at night. The heat hasn't kicked on yet."

Marge offered, "I thought it was squirrels in the attic. We had an infestation of squirrels in my old family house in Arizona. We got used to them. It would have cost too much to get rid of them."

"Well," Tracy added, "here we have an infestation of burglars."

"And we have to learn to live with them," said Alex.

Marge objected, "But that's an unacceptable risk."

"On the contrary," Alex explained, "it's a guarantee of safety. I know of two other spots they use as drop-off points. They treat those spots very carefully. They don't want to upset the status quo. My guess is they broke into the main part of the attic before they discovered this hideaway room. And there's no way they'd hit the rest of the attic again. This is too perfect. Easy access for them and separate from the rest of the house. Just leave well enough alone. And when they've found what they're looking for or when these waters are fished out, they'll move on."

"Weird," said Patti. "Way too weird."

"Better the enemy you know," Alex added.

"That makes no sense to me," Marge insisted. "Sharing an apartment with a bunch of strangers—okay. I think I'm a reasonable judge of people. I can accept that risk. But going about my business like everything's normal when I know that burglars use the attic to store contraband and are coming and going at all hours of the night—no way."

Tom tried to reassure her. "So we'll put a lock on the trap door. So we'll only go up here to the attic in daylight. So we leave alone this room I hadn't used in years."

"No, we call the cops," said Marge.

"Think about it," Alex countered. "What will the cops do? Either they'll take away the stolen goods and anger the burglars. Or they'll try to set a trap and anger the burglars. As long as the burglars don't know that we know, they'll be quiet and careful—model non-paying tenants. If they figure we're on to them and trying to nail them, they might retaliate. And that's a risk I wouldn't want to live with."

"We should call the cops," Marge pursued. "It's our civic duty. With our help they could put an end to this nonsense."

"Tracy," Alex asked, "when you talked to the cops last night did they strike you like they seriously wanted to eradicate this problem?"

"No. I'd say they were just annoyed that it kept happening again and again. They just wanted it to go away."

"So they weren't likely to set up and pull off an elaborate trap?" Tom interrupted, "Even if they wanted to do that, there's the problem that it isn't a single burglar. There are copycats. These three neat stacks of similar stuff tell me that there's at least three of them, or three separate groups of them using this room and cooperating with one another, respecting one another's rights. So if the cops caught one or two or even more of them, there'd be others on the loose. And I wouldn't want to think that there were criminals with a grudge against us and the house that we live in. Random violence, so long as the odds are long, I can live with. That's part of living in a city. But I can't stand the thought of someone deliberately out to get us. I'm with Alex on this one. Leave well enough alone."

7 ~ Five is Company

That night, Tom went to Flanagan's with Tracy and watched the Red Sox game while she worked. When they got back to the apartment, Marge was on the sofa in the kitchen by the big screen TV. She was watching Alfred Hitchcock movies.

The Sox had won. The attic seemed secure from burglars. The embarrassment of Tracy meeting Marge and Patti was over. And this bizarre day was ending with the general expectation that Tracy and he would spend the night together in his room.

But the movie was *Vertigo*, one of Tracy's favorites. And while Tom hinted broadly that they should go to bed, Tracy microwaved some popcorn, took a Fresca from the refrigerator, and settled down on the sofa next to Marge, like she was wide wake and ready to enjoy a medley of old movies, and like she was one of the gang who had lived here forever.

Tom tried another tack. He sat on the arm of the sofa next to Tracy and told her, "Hitchcock is great. But anything but *Vertigo*."

"Are you afraid of heights?" she laughed, incredulous.

"One summer I went to the Grand Canyon with Diane and the kids—to the North Slope. I got dizzy even sitting in the living room of the main lodge, looking out through the picture window at the mile high drop."

"That's silly," insisted Tracy. "You can get rid of fears like that. Just force yourself to face it a few times. Will power."

"But this wasn't just a fear of heights. More like a pull, like a whirlpool that could pull me down. Diane and Laurel and Mark hiked all the trails and loved it. I stayed behind the walls and windows. Thank God for walls and windows."

"I know what you mean," Marge chimed in. "I grew up with that feeling—the pull of imminent danger. My folks loved the Grand Canyon and went camping there every year. It was less than fifty miles from our home. My fear never went away, but I came to love the Canyon despite the fear or because of it—the Canyon was always alive to me—alive with danger."

Tom took Tracy's hand and coaxed her toward the bedroom.

She pulled her hand back and told him, "You go on ahead, Tom. I'll join you soon."

He went to his room, but left the door open a crack, as an invitation, as a reminder that she should join him soon. He lay there for what felt like hours, trying to stay awake. When he woke up at 2 a.m., the television was off. But still no Tracy. He got up to see what was happening, but as he got near the door, he heard Tracy talking—softly to avoid disturbing the sleepers, but animated and non-stop. Rather than open the door, he listened.

Tracy was telling about her life in Kansas before coming to Boston, about her ex-husband who, like her, was a teacher at a junior college at the same school. She divorced him because he was playing around with one of his students. After the divorce, with the two of them still teaching there, she was tempted, in revenge, to have an affair with a student of hers. She had blatantly flirted with a guy about the same age as Alex.

"We got close, very close. Then some trigger went off, and I ran the other way—all the way to Boston. I always had a thing for younger men. That's a weakness I'm trying to correct. I needed a change of scene, a fresh start. I visited Meeghan—a friend of a friend—in Boston. She was going to move out West. I got her old job at Flanagan's.

"I decided that if and when I got close to another man, it would be someone older than me. Tom's perfect—physically older, but child-like in how he responds to me.

"By the way, Marge, I needed a room and I saw Tom's ad. It was just chance that I didn't asked him before you called. I could have wound up living here. And if I had, I'd have never considered going out with him."

"Well, you seem made for each other," Marge offered. "He told us how the two of you hit it off that first time—staying up all night talking."

"Oh, that was fun, but not all that special. I work the late shift; so I'm used to staying up all night after work and sleeping all day. By the way, I shouldn't tell you this, but what the hell—he has a thing for you."

"And what makes you think that?"

"In bed this afternoon, when he was half-asleep, he called me 'Marge' by mistake."

***

Tom woke to a tongue probing his ear and the whispered words, "You naughty little boy. You were listening at the door. You heard all our secrets."

They made love on the floor and then on the mattress.

"You know Meeghan?" Tom asked.

"Yes, I crashed at her place when I arrived in Boston.

"Did she say anything about me?"

"Maybe. I don't think so. I didn't know you then, so I wouldn't have made the connection and remembered. Were you close?"

"No, no. Just Flanagan's. I spent a lot of time in Flanagan's after I was laid off, and even before."

***

Patti had a class early on Saturday morning. As a freshman registering late for the first semester, she was stuck with classes and times that no one else wanted. Spooked by the talk of burglars, she asked Alex to walk her there.

Tracy slept late. So Tom found himself alone with Marge for the first time since she arrived at his door. While Marge did the dishes, Tom put a lock on the trap door—a simple bolt and barrel lock that wouldn't require a key or combination but should prevent anyone from entering the apartment from the attic.

Balanced on the step ladder, with his back to her, he realized she was staring at him—not angry, just curious. Maybe his relationship with Tracy made him interesting or even desirable to her. He couldn't fathom how women think.

He tried to sound casual, "What did you two talk about last night?"

"She did all the talking. Can't say I remember much of it. Our visit to the attic triggered memories of my childhood in Arizona, and the attic in my family's home there—playing hide-and-seek with friends, using old clothes for dress-up games."

"And making out with boy friends?"

"Yes, that too, like you and Diane. For me it was Zeke." She settled down on the sofa and stared up at the trap door to the attic, remembering. Tom figured she had wanted to talk about her memories last night, but Tracy hadn't given her an opening. He sat on the arm of the sofa and gave her his full attention.

"When Zeke and I were sixteen he looked much older than his years. He was over six feet, with a long black beard—like he'd stepped out of a tintype, the image of an old-time Mormon patriarch with a dozen wives. His physical presence, his self-assurance, and his obvious lust for me were turn-ons. I wanted to abandon myself to him, to obey him, to serve him. If I belonged to him, I'd be completely free—I wouldn't have to make decisions, I would have no doubts about my future, or about the meaning and purpose of my life.

"I remember our first time, there in the attic. Despite his assurances that he loved me, that we were destined for one another, and in God's eyes we were married already, the fear of being caught and the sense of sin heightened my senses and my pleasure. I've never felt that kind of intensity since."

She paused, and Tom stayed respectfully silent, not sure how far she wanted to carry this.

"I still sometimes have dreams of my controlling, unforgiving father—an older edition of Zeke. Dad had an uncanny instinct for trouble—popping up whenever I was doing something I shouldn't. Soon after I finally fell asleep last night, I woke up seeing Dad's face the way he looked when he caught me making love with Zeke in the attic.

"I haven't been back in sixteen years. I connect the old house with Mom's death and Dad's discipline. In some ways, that house was a prison for me from which I escaped—going away to college in Boston, on money Mom left me. On the other hand, events that happened there shaped me. I cherish many of those memories. They are part of the architecture of my mind.

"Zeke and I went to the attic many times over the course of a couple years. To Zeke, what we did wasn't sinful. He talked as if it were sacred, that in some metaphysical sense the act alone, without benefit of ceremony, was as binding as marriage. He acted as if he were in total control of me—that I was his, absolutely and forever. I found that notion both romantic and repulsive. His pleasure and his confidence seemed to grow as we did it again and again, while mine declined. As it became routine and expected, when he acted like this was his right and our destiny, I found myself staring up at the rafters or out the window, while he panted and pounded. I started putting him off, inventing excuses why we couldn't go up to the attic, until we hardly ever went there.

"Then Mom died in a car crash, and I needed to be held and Zeke insisted that he wanted to marry me—with an official Mormon marriage that would 'seal' us together for eternity. I put him off, but was too emotionally drained to say no.

"Mom had always encouraged me to do my best at school so I could go away to college in a big city. She had saved enough to make that possible. But Dad wanted me to marry early, marry a devout and traditional Mormon, like Zeke, and stay put.

"So when Dad caught me and Zeke together up in the attic, I sensed it was a put-up job. Dad's righteous fury was too theatrical. And Zeke's contrite repentance was too stilted, as if he had rehearsed the words, as if he were delighted with the prospect of making me an 'honest woman,' and starting a big family with me. It smelled like a trap.

"I worked that out rationally, like solving an algebra problem, while Dad was still screaming and Zeke begging forgiveness and promising to do the right thing. I mouthed the responses they both wanted to hear, and Zeke cradled me in his arms to comfort me, saying as he often said, 'Easy does it. Easy does it.'

"But a day after, I headed East by bus, with a suitcase full of books—I could buy clothes anywhere—and with a cashier's check for all the money Mom had saved for my education and escape."

After she finished her tale, they sat quietly, Marge still staring up at the trap door to the attic, and Tom watching her, imagining the scenes she had described.

Then Alex rushed in, holding high a small gray rectangle of plastic. "Tracy! Tracy!" he called. "Come and get it."

Tracy stumbled out of Tom's room in nothing but an unbuttoned shirt. "What?"

"Your Kindle is what."

"My Kindle? How could you have my Kindle?"

"Bought it from a street vendor. Just fifty bucks. He had no idea of its value. He didn't even know what it was used for."

"How do you know it's mine?"

He flipped the on-off switch and read from the Main Menu—"J.D. Robb, James Patterson, Anne Rice, Jane Austen, Charlotte Bronte. I'd say that sounds like you."

She grabbed it from him and stared at that menu page. "Good God! That is mine."

She threw her arms around Alex and gave him an enthusiastic kiss on the lips, and lingered there, Tom noted, beyond the boundary of what spontaneous gratitude might merit.

Tom joked, "You ought to go into the detective business."

"That's not for me," Alex objected, taking him literally. "You won't catch me playing cops and robbers with real bullets. And I'm not about to climb fire escapes to snap photos of cheating couples in bed."

"I was thinking more of what seems to be your specialty—recovering stolen property."

"Now that I could do," Alex laughed.

"Then come with me," Tom suggested.

"Where to?"

"To Gold's Gym. I've decided to work out every day, take self-defense lessons, maybe even take Italian cooking classes—become a regular Spenser, from the Robert Parker mysteries. You can be my Hawk."

"Now there's a challenge," Alex answered, taking an attacking martial arts pose aimed at Tracy. "Give me all your Kindles."

"No way, Jose," she answered.

"Okay, Tom," Alex agreed. "You've got a partner. I'll be your loyal bodyguard and side kick until sundown today, so help me Kindle."

***

At the gym, the training was eclectic and pragmatic. No traditional oriental rigamarole. What mattered was what worked, and what would work was different for everyone. The trainer quickly noted, "Tom, that left leg of yours has natural talent. The way you can stretch it and stiffen it, and kick high. That's your bionic leg. Build on that and you'll be a formidable fighter."

"In a few weeks?" Tom prompted.

"A few years, I'd say."

"Maybe a few decades," Alex offered.

Walking home from the gym, Alex led the way, taking them on a route that passed street vendors. Tom had never paid attention to them before, but this time, encouraged by Alex who acted as native guide, Tom looked closely and found a silver plate bowl and matching pitcher with the name "Prudence Case" scratched on the bottom.

Alex kidded, "Maybe you're the one who should go into stolen property recovery."

When Tom started to quibble with the vendor over price, Alex took out his wallet, handed the guy $50—half what he was asking—and the deal was done.

As they approached Tom's building, Tom noticed a couple guys looking closely at the building from the opposite sidewalk. Tom stopped Alex, and they waited ten minutes until those guys moved on.

"I sense something's wrong."

"A paranormal experience?" asked Alex. "Do you have those often? That could come in handy with your investigations."

"More like a paranoid experience, I must admit. But it feels like not just our building, but the whole city is infested with burglars."

***

That evening, Tracy left for work early with Tom. Following a suggestion from Alex, they took a detour down Boylston Street to check the street vendors. Near the Copley Square subway stop, one street vendor was typing rapidly on a wireless laptop. Tom took a peek from behind and delighted in telling Tracy, "You're seeing a high tech fence in action. While displaying his wares on a blanket on the sidewalk, he's posting those same items for sale on eBay, taking the pictures with a cheap cellphone and using the laptop to connect to the Internet. Of course, if he had an iPhone he wouldn't need the laptop. He'll probably upgrade to that next week."

"That could be my laptop," Tracy whispered.

"But nobody took your laptop."

"Not that time. But we haven't been back there for a couple days."

"Same brand?"

"Yes. I wish I could check for my files."

"How much for the laptop?" Tom asked the guy, out loud.

"But it might not be mine," Tracy whispered.

"Then I'll have another laptop to play Free Cell on," Tom answered her. "What's the price?" he asked again.

"Not for sale."

Doing an Alex imitation, Tom took out his wallet, stared the guy in the eye, and announced, "I'll give you three hundred. Cash. No questions."

"Sold."

At Flanagan's, while Tracy did her job, Tom checked the laptop. All the files had been erased except the photos of merchandise. So, there was no telling if it was Tracy's. Her machine might still be sitting on her desk.

After work, they went straight to Tracy's place.

The laptop was missing. Even her clothes were missing. And the floorboards had been torn up.

They left immediately and went back to Tom's place.

Alex explained, "The burglar knew you wouldn't stay around after a scare like that. Or he may have seen you leave the building. So he went right back and finished the job. The clothes he probably ditched in a dumpster. That and tearing up the floor were probably just his idea of revenge for your calling the cops."

"Well, I'll call the cops again, and my landlord," said Tracy. "But not now. In the morning. I've had enough for now. I don't want to think about it."

"What are you going to do?" asked Tom. "Long run."

"Long run? Who knows. All I know is that there's no way I'd ever move back there."

"But ..."

She probed his ear with her tongue and whispered. "Danger is a turn on."

Alex, with an exaggerated gentlemanly bow offered to move into the attic and let Tracy have his room.

"Thanks for the offer," she replied. "but I don't think I'll be needing that." Again she probed Tom's ear with her tongue.

Tom said nothing, but he felt torn. Tracy was so available, so tempting, such a fantasy in the flesh. But he had only known her for a couple weeks. And this felt like a serious commitment. She wanted to move in with him, and he'd have felt foolish—no, idiotic—saying or doing anything to stop her. But he couldn't help but wonder what might have happened between him and Marge under different circumstances.

8 ~ The Gas Man Cometh

On Sunday morning, Tom and Alex headed to the gym, Marge went shopping, Tracy slept in, and Patti settled down in the kitchen to do homework.

As Patti later recounted the events, soon after Marge left, the doorbell rang. Patti rushed to the intercom. This was the first doorbell-ringing visitor they had had since she moved in.

A deep voice announced that he was the "gas man", from National Grid. They were checking all the houses on the block for leaks.

Without hesitation, she buzzed him in.

The gas man, about six foot five, with flab hanging over his belt, wore a dark blue work uniform with National Grid embroidered on the shirt pocket. His belt was heaving with tools, so when he leaned over, the top of his butt crack showed, like a plumber. He looked and acted workmanlike and official; and being friendly, he asked about her roommates—who they were, what they did, where they were now, and which room was whose. Patti, playing the woman of the house—proud that she had been there to let him in and thereby had saved him time and trouble and maybe had helped avert disaster—was open and friendly, answering all his questions. But there were too many questions. She had work to do, and this was getting annoying.

She told him that someone was sleeping in Tom's room and asked that he please not disturb that person unless absolutely necessary. She didn't mention Tracy's name and deliberately didn't indicate her sex or why she was there. That should be no business of his. His chatty chumminess was irritating. It was an invasion of privacy.

Hearing that, he seemed flustered, like an actor who hears an unexpected line and doesn't know what to reply outside of the script. He took out a cell phone as if he wanted a prompt, then put it away, reassumed his official demeanor, and started the inspection.

Patti trailed behind him, uneasy and growing suspicious, but with no concrete reason to doubt he was who he said he was. He checked every room but Tom's—pointing a testing gadget, as if he were a prospector hunting for uranium with a Geiger counter. He looked in every closet, behind every picture on the wall, under every bed, in every cabinet. He inspected for more than an hour, then left.

That evening after she told her tale to Tom, Marge, Alex, and Tracy, Tom asked her sharply, "What kind of stove do we have?"

"Electric."

"And the clothes drier?"

"I don't know. You just push the button, and it works."

"That's electric, too. And we have oil heat. And the hot water also comes from an oil furnace."

"So what's the point?" she asked, annoyed at this barrage of questions and the implication that she had done something wrong.

"There is no gas anywhere in this building. There used to be when the house was built—back in the days of gas lights. But as soon as electricity became available, my great-grandmother Pru insisted the gas lines get taken out. There hasn't been any gas in this house for over a hundred years."

"And how was I supposed to know that?"

"Don't be so trusting. You're living in the city. We think we have burglars in the attic, but that isn't the only risk. Any stranger could be a rapist, or a murderer or Lord knows what. You need to be on your guard at all times, for your sake and for ours as well.

Marge added, "Even if we used gas, you shouldn't buzz somebody in just because he says he's a gas man. You call the gas company first to confirm that they sent someone."

"But I told him I wasn't alone, and I didn't tell him it was a man or a woman. I was cautious."

"That much was good. But you were far too trusting," Marge insisted.

"You could have put Tracy at risk as well as yourself," added Alex.

"But he didn't do anything wrong," Patti pleaded.

Alex explained, "He was probably casing the place, planning to come back later, maybe with others."

"You guys sound so paranoid."

"And for good reason," Tom insisted. "He claimed he needed to inspect the building, but apparently he only checked this apartment. He didn't look for and inspect gas pipes—there were none. Instead, he looked in every closet and cabinet, and even behind pictures. He was ridiculously thorough, but he didn't need to check my room—it wasn't important enough for him to disturb whoever was sleeping there. If you had just thought it out logically—"

"I would have totally freaked. I can't live that way—assuming the worst about everyone."

"You're a small-town girl. You need to learn how to live safely in a city," Marge urged. "You need to be careful with strangers wherever you go, even walking to school. Tom's right—it isn't just burglars you need to worry about. You have to be careful how you dress, who you make eye contact with, where you walk, even how you walk."

"Loose hips sink ships," Tracy offered.

"Exactly," Marge affirmed.

Alex offered, "If you felt uncomfortable—and it sounds like you did—you could call any of us on our cell phones."

"As if I know your numbers."

"We should enter them all on one another's phones now."

While they were doing that, Tom, on impulse, picked up the receiver of the landline phone, which was lying on the kitchen counter. He put it back in its cradle, then picked it up again, and dialed a code. Then he frowned and put the receiver down again, not in its cradle.

"What's wrong?" asked Marge.

"I thought I'd check the voicemail, but there are too many messages."

"How many?"

"Two hundred sixteen. I don't want to deal with that right now."

"Well, you'll have to sooner or later."

"Later. Much later. I have no desire to listen to all those apartment seekers with their sad stories and pleas."

Alex offered, "There's probably some code to erase them all, without having to listen to them."

"But there could be something important," Marge objected. "A message from your kids or your ex-wife. Some emergency."

"I'm in no mood for emergencies right now."

"Well, a job offer then."

"Not likely," Tom chuckled grimly. "For weeks I've been waiting for that phone to ring—and nothing, absolutely nothing. When you're waiting like that, the silence can be nerve-wracking. It's much better knowing that it can't ring."

Patti suggested, "But you never know—like the gas man."

"That wasn't a gas man," Tom insisted.

"But there could be a message from that person or his company, saying he was coming and explaining why. It may have been a simple, innocent misunderstanding. Besides you can't—"

"Can't what? Can't leave my phone off the hook? Nobody's paying me to be on call. It's been relaxing these last few days—not just the phone not ringing, but knowing it wasn't going to ring. What does it matter anyway? You all have cell phones. Nobody's affected but me."

"That sounds logical," Marge admitted. "But it makes me feel uncomfortable. I feel there's some social contract that says you should always be reachable."

Tom chuckled, "Sure, Marge, and aren't you the one who first noticed the phone was off the hook and left it that way?"

"Okay, so I'm responsible. So if it's all right with you, Tom, I'll listen to all the messages, delete the ones that sound useless, and save any that might be important."

"Be my guest."

It was nearly midnight when Marge got to the end of the messages, and she only saved the last one—a message that had come in while she was listening to and deleting the rest.

Patti was doing her homework, and Tom was checking the Web in the kitchen. They both watched anxiously as Marge listened to it over and over again, getting more disturbed each time.

"An emergency?" asked Tom.

Marge waved him off.

"Is the voice hard to understand?" asked Patti.

"Here. Listen to it yourself," Marge hit the speaker-phone button, and the replay code.

The voice was muffled as if spoken through a piece of cloth and with a phony-sounding Indian accent.

"Marge, Marge, why don't you pick up the phone? I know you're there, Marge."

"What's strange about that?" asked Patti. "It's just someone trying to reach you."

"But I didn't give this number to anyone. Anyone who knows me would call me on my cell phone."

"Unless ..." Alex offered.

"Unless what?"

"Unless someone wanted to freak you out. Unless he wanted to prove to you that he knows who you are and where you are and what you're up to."

"Jack?" Marge asked in disbelief. "That couldn't be Jack."

"Jack?" asked Patti.

"My ex. The boyfriend I moved out on."

"Creepy," noted Patti.

"We broke up a few weeks ago, and I haven't spoken to him since. There's no way he could know this number. And if he really wanted to talk to me, he'd just use my cell. And that's definitely not his voice."

"Maybe he had someone else make the call for him," suggested Tom.

"Even creepier," Patti concluded.

9 ~ Such a Nice Couple

The next morning, while Marge and Tom relaxed at the kitchen table, reading the morning news and sipping coffee, the phone rang.

Marge jumped up and spilled her coffee, narrowly missing the keyboard of her computer. Patti and Tracy were still in bed, and Alex was missing. His door was open. His room was empty. And no one had seen or heard from him since last night

The phone rang again.

Maybe it was Alex. Marge reached for the phone, then hesitated.

It rang a third time.

She picked it up.

"Hello. Yes. I'll get him. Tom! It's for you. A woman."

Tom took the phone. "Hello. Yes, that's the woman I'm living with," he winked at Marge. "No, I guess that's not entirely accurate. She's one of the women I'm living with." He winked again. "Yes, harems can be fun." He hung up. "That was Diane. She hung up on me. I wish I could have seen her face." He sounded pleased with himself.

"Well, maybe I should give Jack this number so he can call and hear you pick up." Marge smiled.

***

When Tom got home from a long day of workouts and lessons at the gym, he found Alex sitting with his laptop at the kitchen table. Tom didn't know what to say to him, and Alex didn't volunteer an explanation for his absence. Tom, having spent a night away himself, with no warning and no call, couldn't complain.

Marge, who had no such constraints, attacked. "You act as if dropping completely out of sight, with no explanation, is as normal as coffee with breakfast. You act as if you're a guest in this apartment, as if you have no responsibilities to the rest of us. We need to establish a schedule and chores, and you're off God-knows-where."

"Supper," Alex interjected.

"What? You expect—"

Alex laughed. "No, I'm volunteering. If you're giving out chores, I'll take supper. I'll cook supper every night for all of us."

"You cook?"

"Actually, I'm quite good at it. But you can judge that for yourself tomorrow when I have my premiere."

Then, the phone rang again.

Patti and Tracy popped out of their rooms.

It rang again.

Patti took hold of Marge's hand and Alex's and squeezed.

It rang again.

Tom stood up and the others looked at him expectantly. But instead of walking toward the phone, he backed away from it.

It rang again, and Marge extricated her hand from Patti's grip and bolted toward the phone to pick it up before it switched to voice mail.

Once she heard, she smiled in relief and said, "Patti, it's for you."

Patti, puzzled and hesitant, took the phone from her, listened for a second, then hung up.

"There was no one there," she explained. "Just a dial tone. Marge, who was it?"

"I don't know. Just a voice, a woman's voice. She said, 'Can I speak to Patti please?' That's all. There was nothing suspicious about it."

"But I didn't give that number to anyone."

"Are you sure it was a woman?" asked Alex.

"Are you into conspiracy theories?" Marge laughed nervously.

"Are you sure?" he repeated.

"It was too quick. I didn't expect .... No, I'm not sure. It might have been a man disguising his voice. He, I mean she, said so little."

"What about caller ID?" asked Tom.

"It says private number."

***

That night Tom fell asleep at his table at Flanagan's, and Tracy shooed him home. The work-outs and his turned-around sleep schedule had exhausted him. Tracy was going to try to switch to the day shift. She and

Tom needed to get their routines in order. As he drifted off, alone on his mattress, he heard Patti and Alex in the kitchen.

"And what exactly do you do for income?" Patti asked.

"I make deals."

"What kind of deals?"

"I do favors for one guy so I can get favors from another. A little of this. A little of that."

"You sound like the Godfather when he started out—a favor here, a favor there."

"Good business practice. People networking."

"And that guy, the gas man, did he maybe object to some of the favors you've been doing? Was he maybe an enemy of your networking friends? Was he doing someone a favor by going after you?"

"You have dramatic flair, Patti. You should try creative writing. BU has a great creative writing program run by the novelist Leslie Epstein."

"And I suppose he owes you a few favors?"

"No, but he should consider it a favor if I send a beautiful and talented young lady in his direction, someone who will bring acclaim to the department."

"Can you say that to my face?"

"That's what I'm doing."

"I mean, look me in the eye when you talk to me."

"Sure, sis," he readily agreed. "Such beautiful eyes. When I'm looking at you like this, it's all too easy for me to forget what I wanted to say."

"Cut the BS, Alex. It's out of character."

"And you know me so well, sis," he chuckled.

"What are you afraid of?"

He hesitated, then smiled nervously and answered, "Gargamel and Greedy Smurf, just like you."

***

That night Alex cooked for the first time—spaghetti with a sauce including ground beef, sausage, fresh tomatoes, mozzarella, onion, and raisins—lots of raisins. Patti went overboard in her praise. Tom and Marge tried to avoid comment. Alex beamed with pride and served second helpings to all, not noticing Tom and Marge's distress. He was proud of the recipe, which he had thought up himself. He offered to teach Tom Italian cooking.

Tom suggested instead, "Maybe we both should take that cooking course at Boston Adult Ed."

Then the doorbell rang.

"Oh shit," Patti exclaimed.

"Gas men don't come at night," said Tom.

"Even people pretending to be gas men don't come at night," added Marge.

Alex quietly edged his way toward the trapdoor to the attic.

"No. No," Patti protested. "With the gas man and everything, I forgot. I meant to tell you that George is coming."

"George?"

"That's my dad, my dad George, my birth mother's second ex. I live with him and his new wife Mary. He's bringing my stuff."

"And probably, finally, he's checking your new living arrangement," added Marge.

"Yes, and no. Yes, he is checking. But no, he doesn't feel uncomfortable about it. He figures this is a lot better than the dorms."

"Really? What did you tell him?" Marge asked.

"Well, he kind of has the impression that you two are a couple."

"And you didn't disillusion him?" asked Tom.

"Explaining would have been awkward, and he'll only be here a short while. I can explain later if I need to. Why make him feel uncomfortable now? At the slightest hint that there were two adults here, he guessed that your kids had grown up and moved out—like Tom's did—and your way of dealing with the empty nest was to take in college students as roomers. He sounded proud of himself for understanding the situation so well."

"Very logical," Tom noted.

"So could you please, for my sake, look and act like a couple now? You don't need to lie or anything, just play along with what he assumes already."

Tom put his arm around Marge's shoulder.

Marge tried not to cringe.

Alex pulled his cell phone out of his pocket and snapped a picture, "All you need is a pitchfork to look like American Gothic."

"Perfect," Patti concluded. "It's a good thing Tracy is at work. You and Tracy wouldn't have been credible as a couple—not a married couple anyway."

Tom looked puzzled.

Marge laughed.

Alex and Tom helped George carry up a trunk and five suitcases.

"How did you get all this stuff together?" Alex asked him.

"Patti had already packed most of it before she left for Europe, when she thought she'd be going to the U. of Michigan. Then she gave me a list of extras—about three suitcases worth—over the phone."

"Speaking of extras, which suitcase has my t-shirts?"

George handed it to her, and she quickly carried it into her room.

As soon as she closed her door, George exclaimed, "God! Is that how they dress in college now?"

Marge quickly replied, "Not all of them, from what I can tell. At least not yet. I think she picked up that look on her trip to Europe."

"I dread to think what else she may have learned there. It's not easy being a parent these days, as you well know."

"Hey, I heard that," Patti called from her room. "No fair conspiring."

She couldn't have asked for a better outcome. George totally bought the idea of Marge and Tom as a married couple. It was like he was passing them the baton of parental responsibility.

"How many kids do you have?" asked George.

"Two," Tom answered quickly, and gave Marge a quick hug. "Laurel and Mark are just a few years older than these two. When they moved out, the house felt so empty."

Patti was delighted. He was playing the part just as she had hoped he would.

"I know what you mean. We started feeling it as soon as Patti left for Europe. I think it might be worse for surrogate parents like us than for real ones like you. We're parents by choice, rather than by chance."

Patti came out in a too-tight, too-short tee-shirt that said, "I'd rather be guiling," drawing attention to a bust that needed no enhancement.

"God," George exclaimed again. "She is a handful. Thank God she isn't walking around the streets of Plymouth dressed like that."

"I don't think she should walk around the streets of Boston like that either," Marge added, with a judgmental frown.

"I just can't make sense of kids these days. Mary and I talk about it all the time. What's the right thing to do? How can we help set her on the right track? There's one boy in particular who was always hanging around—more a stalker than a boyfriend."

"Reggie?" Patti countered. "He's harmless."

"Well, I'm not sure how harmless he is. But I must admit I was relieved to see you off to Europe. I don't think I could have taken another hot summer with a town full of hormone-crazed boys staring at you; and Reggie, in particular, creeping around. He hasn't called you here has he?"

"No," she said quickly.

As if on cue, the phone rang.

Tom and Marge and Alex and Patti looked at one another, but no one went to pick it up. After four rings, it stopped.

"Reggie doesn't have that number," Patti mumbled.

Tom explained, "I'm sure it's a telemarketer. They call every night about this time. Besides, these days the only real calls come by cell phone. It's probably time I cancelled the land-line service."

"It's the same even in our small town in New Hampshire," George chimed in. "Almost as bad as spam on the Internet."

"But, Tom, we can't just let it ring like that," Marge urged. "There's no telling when it will be important."

"If you care so much, then you should answer it, dear."

"No. We should make answering the phone a chore, like shopping for groceries and cooking dinner."

Alex piped in proudly, "Dinner, that's me."

"I do the dishes," added Tom.

"And what's Patti's chore?"

She answered from her room, "I mop the kitchen floor and put out the trash."

"Excellent. Mary and I were never organized enough for chores. When Patti first came to live with us—she was fourteen and a freshman in high school—we didn't want to set up anything that could get in the way of her studies or her making friends in her new school. And by the time we realized that she could get A's without seeming to work, and that she made friends in a wink, we'd already established habits, and it would have been awkward to impose chores, and, besides, she was so happy the way things were."

"Speaking of supper," Alex interjected. "Please join us. I made spaghetti tonight, and there's enough for another half-dozen people."

"Yes," Marge added, with a touch of irony that Alex missed, "please spare us from leftovers."

George loved it—especially the raisins. He took three helpings and wrote down the recipe that Alex was anxious to share.

Alex explained that he was an only-child of busy parents and had eaten take out from restaurants most of the time when he was a kid. When he was off on his own, he experimented cooking for himself, and now he looked forward to having an audience for his culinary creations.

George admitted that the last couple weeks had been difficult for Mary and him. They wanted to come rushing down to Boston and make sure Patti made the right choices. It's so hard to strike the right balance— letting her be herself and learn how to cope in the real world, trying not to be over-protective, but wanting to make sure she's safe. Patti had insisted that they wait until she had her room in order before coming. Today was the earliest she would allow. Mary was minding the store today, while he did the last-minute packing and drove on down.

"Store? What kind of store?" Alex asked immediately.

Soon George was explaining the antique business and the impact the Internet was having, both as a new outlet for him—a way for him to reach new and distant customers—and as a way competitors could get at his traditional local customer base.

Alex took notes, and George evidently loved the attention. Patti couldn't have been more pleased with Alex's performance, though she wasn't sure if it was a performance, or just Alex being Alex, whoever that was.

Alex advised that George set up an eBay store, not just sell separate items at open auctions. He could and should sell some items at a fixed price, rather than by bid—the kinds of things that he usually had in stock and could readily replace. In any case, having an eBay store would give him the benefit of free automatic cross-promotion on all his auctions.

"That Alex is amazing," George told Patti when saying goodbye at the street door. "What he just told me could help boost my business 10%, maybe even 20%. And Marge and Tom are such a nice couple."

They all got a chuckle out that of last line when Patti told them.

10 ~ To Dorm or Not to Dorm

Patti was the next one not to come home at night. Tracy eventually sorted out what had happened and explained it to Tom.

Patti's college expectations were based mainly on what she had heard from her various parents. She discounted what she had seen in movies and TV series as Hollywood nonsense. And, she figured that what she had seen on college visits was atypical.

For two weeks, she acted like a typical freshman—self-conscious, curious, anxious, running on adrenalin. Then two decisions, prompted by Becky and Alex, changed her.

Becky sat next to Patti in freshman English. She presumed that Patti felt "out of it" living off campus, so she told Patti everything that was happening in the dorms to make her feel involved in campus life.

After class late on the Friday afternoon of the second week of classes, Becky asked, "Do you have a lease?"

"No."

"Did you pay a security deposit?"

"No, just the first month's rent. Tom said he didn't see the need for a security deposit."

"That's great. That means you're free—unlike just about every other freshman living off campus. Sure, lots of people who didn't get in the dorms have made deals they can't get out of or only can at too much cost. But you've got a shot—a real shot."

"A shot at what?"

"One of my roommates just moved out. 'Money matters' she said. Her dad lost his job, and she's going to commute from the suburbs to save money. She had to move fast to get as much of a refund as possible. That means there's an opening. And of all the freshmen who might want it, you're probably the first to hear of it, and you're one of the very few who isn't tied up with a lease and can actually move in."

"But—"

"But what? Go for it! Pack an overnight bag. Come sleep in the dorm tonight. The housing office won't be open until Monday anyway. Stay for the weekend. Meet my other roommates—Jillian and Rachel—and the other girls and guys on our floor. You'll love it. They'll love you. It's perfect."

Before Patti could plead for time to think, Becky was off to a drama club meeting, assuming that Patti would meet her at her dorm by six—in time for all the roommates to have dinner together.

Patti walked back to the apartment slowly, by a roundabout route. She was disoriented. Just a couple weeks ago she would have been ecstatic about an opportunity to move into the dorms.

But she felt comfortable with Tom and Marge and Alex and Tracy. She had fallen into a daily routine that felt good. She liked these people. The fact that Tom hadn't tied her up with legal documents and security deposits didn't mean that she was free. It meant that she had a moral obligation. He had trusted her—a total stranger. And she had made a verbal commitment to him. To her, that was more important than legalisms.

But she had always dreamt of living in a college dorm. How could she turn down the chance that had fallen her way so miraculously? It was like getting accepted to BU off the waiting list—when the chance came, you had to grab it. Or, at least she had to seriously consider it. She owed that much to herself, no matter how much she owed, in a moral sense, to Tom and Marge and Alex and Tracy. And how much could that be after just a couple weeks? And with so many people having called about Tom's room rental, he could replace her quickly. In another week or two they'd have forgotten her.

But how could she tell them she wanted to move out? Or even tell them about the sleepover/test drive?

Patti felt she needed to ask Tom and Marge—especially Marge—for permission to sleep somewhere else tonight and tomorrow night. She remembered her own reaction when Tom and then Alex stayed out all night without warning. And this would be two nights in a row. And the way George hit it off with Marge and Tom, he presumed he had handed the parental baton to them. And what with the burglaries and the gas man incident, they'd be sure to worry.

She was on her own. There were no official rules. She didn't need anyone's permission to sleep over. But she felt she should tell them where she was going.

Marge would be the one who would draw conclusions first, and probably accurate ones. She'd guess right away that Patti was thinking about moving out.

Marge was in the kitchen when Patti walked in and blurted out the excuse that her aunt in Providence was sick and she needed to go visit her for the weekend.

Marge gave her a puzzled look, then asked, "So you met a guy that quickly?"

"What?"

"It seems fast to me. The old fashioned way would be to go to a few movies together, take a few walks in the park, go to lunch, go out to dinner, and talk a lot, before you shack up for a weekend."

"I'm not going off to sleep with a guy."

"A girl then?"

"You have the wrong idea entirely."

"Okay. I don't understand. And I'm not your mother. But if you didn't feel uncomfortable about what you're doing—whatever you're doing— you wouldn't come up with such a lame excuse. You wouldn't feel you needed to make up an excuse at all. Actually, I'm flattered. It's like you're asking me for my blessing—giving an excuse as transparent as that, knowing that I'll know it isn't true, and hoping I'll say, 'Yes, of course. You're on your own now. You have every right to do what you want. How considerate of you to spend your weekend taking care of a sick aunt. Please give my regards to her.' Amazing. I've never felt so much like a mother in my life."

Patti was too confused and angry to reply. She packed a suitcase, put on a t-shirt with a message that suited her mood, *I'd rather be wildering*, and walked out.

***

On her first day of classes, Patti had only seen a couple of others dressed like her in what she thought of as *Euro style*.

A week later, a couple dozen other students had started dressing that way. By the Friday night of the second week of classes, the night of the sleep over at the dorm, just about everyone—including Becky and her other future roommates—had adopted that style.

When they went to supper—walking across the street from the Warren Towers to the Student Union—Jillian and Rachel and Becky were all with guys. Patti didn't catch their names—she was meeting too many new people at once. The town she came from had a population of less than three thousand, and BU had over thirty thousand students—that change took some getting used to.

At supper, sandwiches at D'Angelo's, an extra guy showed up, sat down next to Patti and acted like he was part of the group. He talked a lot. His name was Ollie. He was on the football team, a junior. He was in her freshman English class, taking it for the second or third time. She had vague recollections of someone as big and tall as him, following her around campus.

Back at the dorm, many of the suites had their doors open, with loud music and beer for the taking. Becky, Jillian, Rachel and the boys who were with them encouraged Patti to join in the party.

That night, Patti's period came on suddenly, early. Fortunately there was a tampon dispenser in the co-ed bathroom next to the condom dispenser. But when she came out, her friends—all but Ollie—had disappeared. Patti wandered the halls, peeking in one suite after another, looking for them. Ollie shadowed her everywhere, always a beer in hand. She thought, *Shouldn't a football player be in training?*

When she ignored him, he smiled. When she was rude to him, he smiled. When she told him to "get lost," he smiled even more. When she went out to buy a large Coke with lots of ice, he followed her. When she needed to use the bathroom to change her tampon, he followed her in and leaned on a sink while she went into a stall. She couldn't take it anymore. Enough was enough. When she came out, she gave him a hug, and loosening his belt she dumped all the ice from her drink down his pants.

He bellowed and danced and dropped his trousers.

She dashed into a nearby dorm room and hid until he had lumbered away, cursing loudly.

Hours later, when she found her way back to Becky's suite—her future home—she found some guy she had never seen before asleep on her bed. And on the other bed in the room, Jillian was cuddled under the covers with some guy—not the same one she was with at supper.

Patti went back out to the common room of the suite, turned off the TV, wiped up spills from the orange plastic sofa, turned off the half dozen lights, stuffed facial tissue in her ears to reduce the noise from nearby suites, and made herself as comfortable as she could.

***

When she woke up a few hours later at dawn, with sunlight streaming through the windows, which had neither shades nor curtains, she fetched her suitcase and left without saying a word to anyone.

Drowsy, she took a couple of wrong turns, but eventually found her way back to the apartment on Fairfield Street. She could have sworn that someone was staring at her and following her, someone as big as Ollie. But he walked away whenever she turned, and she didn't get a good look at him.

When she arrived at the apartment, at about seven in the morning, Alex was already working on his laptop at the kitchen table.

"What's his name?" he asked before even saying hello.

"Marge told you?"

"She made it the main topic of discussion at dinner last night."

"She's wrong."

"But she's so proud of herself for having you pegged. It would be cruel to disillusion her, even worse to prove her wrong. She means well. Let her win this one, or think she won."

"Okay, okay. I'll admit to her that I didn't go visit a sick aunt. I'll tell her I was with a football player named Ollie, who was a drunken idiot. When I couldn't stand to be with him anymore, I headed straight home."

"That's a good story. Much better than the aunt thing. Much more worthy of your creative abilities. So what really happened?"

"Okay, already."

And that was when she made her second decision.

11 ~ Advanced Placement

When she told Alex about Ollie and ice cubes, he quipped, "The attack of the Ice Maiden," and laughed so loud she was afraid he'd wake Marge and Tom.

"I'm sure there was no permanent damage," she emphasized.

"But if he bellowed in a dorm full of party-goers, your handiwork and his humiliation are public knowledge. Methinks you're going to need a bodyguard, fair lady."

His ironic look and manner reminded her of Michel, the French tour guide she met while backpacking in Europe last summer. She had heard him delivering his spiel to his group in the Musée d'Orsay . She had followed along. When he was talking about the Impressionists, their eyes met. He smiled. He knew very well she wasn't part of his group. So she stayed put while the group moved on to the next room. But he looked back at her and waved her on. "Come on, Madeline," he called. "We don't have all day." When it was time for the group to get on the bus, he waved her on again, and introduced her to the rest of the group as "Madeline St. James from Detroit, a late entry to the group." When they got to the hotel, he took her out to dinner, alone, then escorted her to the pension where she was staying. At his prompting, she rejoined the group the next morning, and the next. On the third night, she moved into his hotel room.

Patti presumed that, as in the case of Michel, Alex's irony and detachment were Byronic—that he had a history of heartbreak. But she couldn't ask Alex about his past or he would change the subject, tell her how creative she was, and once again encourage her to take that writing course, which maybe she should.

She had Advancement Placement credits in English, History, and French, but she hadn't exercised them because her acceptance had come so late that she hadn't had time to think about course choices. Besides, she was in awe of BU. She had figured she'd be at a disadvantage relative to other students because she came from a backwoods town. The others would all be better prepared. She'd be best off taking freshman courses.

As Patti told Alex, after two weeks in class and part of a weekend in a dorm, her opinion of her classmates had dropped precipitously. She contrasted the dorm lifestyle, with its non-stop noise and distractions and the family-like lifestyle she had here in the apartment. She explained what she felt about the behavior of Ollie and Becky, her disappointment in her classes and her classmates, and how she had expected college to be so much more challenging.

Gradually, she talked herself into wanting to get into that creative writing class. And if she was doing that, she should try to get out of other freshman lecture courses. She had already heard great things about a history seminar on the Cold War and a French seminar on political themes in contemporary literature. She was now convinced she could do that level of work, and she should.

But she'd have to move fast, and the school bureaucracy was daunting. No, she decided, it was too late; she'd have to make do with what she had.

Back and forth she flip-flopped, talking out-loud to herself, with her head resting on Alex's shoulder as they sat on the edge of his bed.

Finally, he reassured her that he had connections who could help with the paperwork. She shouldn't worry. He'd take care of it all.

She believed him. She finally relaxed.

She woke up in the dark—on his bed, fully clothed, under the covers. He was sleeping on the floor nearby.

She got up quietly, kissed him on the forehead, and went to her own room.

She slept all through Saturday.

She had anticipated having to explain to Marge and Tom why she came back on Saturday. Now she would sleep late on Sunday and no explanation should be necessary.

She dreamt that a faceless stalker, the same height and build as Ollie, followed her to and from school, waiting for the odd moment when she was off-guard. She woke up in a sweat, went back into Alex's room and woke him and told him. He gave her all the reassurance she could have wanted. He volunteered to walk her to school and meet her at the library in the late afternoon to walk her home for as long as she wanted. He told her he didn't think it was necessary. His comment about the need for a "bodyguard" had been a joke. But his schedule was flexible; he could use some exercise; and he would enjoy her company.

She went back to bed.

***

Patti woke up Sunday at noon, rested and refreshed, and determined to change her life. Not only would she, with Alex's help, switch to upper-level courses, but she would also change her style of dress—and that would be a reminder of her new direction.

She put on a t-shirt with the slogan *I'd rather be having,* and, without breakfast or lunch, without a word to anyone, set out for the clothing stores on Newbury and Boylston Streets. She wanted *Father Knows Best* and *Donna Reed* clothes—the 50's look. She struck out at one store after another before she found what she wanted in a thrift shop. She bought everything they had of the kind.

She had so many bags she needed to take a cab home. Once inside her room, she started dressing in front of the full-length mirror on her door, trying one combination after another until she had created half a dozen outfits that felt just right.

Then she fetched an iron and ironing board that she had noticed in the attic. Her mother Mary had once shown her how to iron when getting ready for a Halloween party. It was hard to believe that once upon a time people actually did this for all their clothes every time they washed them. She felt like a time traveler.

When she emerged from her room into the kitchen, Alex was cooking dinner, and Marge was coming out of her room.

Patti was wearing a knee-length woolen pleated red-and-blue plaid skirt, a loose-fitting frilly white blouse, and knee-high red socks. A red ribbon went from the top of head, behind her ears and under her hair at the back, pulling it up a bit, so it bounced as she walked.

The new look was so retro, prim, and proper, it was perfect—so perfect that Marge stared in disbelief.

"My aunt had the wildest old outfits," Patti explained. "I couldn't help but play dress-up. And then she insisted that I bring some of them home."

She wished she had had her camera with her to capture Marge's reaction to that line.

Patti dressed that way for school the next day, and for the next couple weeks. She noticed a few others trying to imitate the look. But no one else found the "real thing".

She also noticed that with the new look she drew just as much attention from the guys as she had with the old one.

12 ~ The Times They Are a Changing

After another week, Tracy's day-shift became part of the household routine. Tom walked Tracy to Flanagan's in the morning, went to the gym for workouts and lessons, read in the breaks, then met Tracy to walk home with her at dinner time. Alex often tagged along. Tom no longer bothered to look for jobs. And Alex still hadn't divulged his source of income. Alex kept irregular hours, spent a lot of time on the Web, and every now and then didn't come home at night.

Tracy was suspicious. "The gas man and those phone calls could all have been about Alex," she insisted. "And he found that Kindle of mine awfully fast."

Tom, too, wondered, and occasionally asked Alex about his line of work. Then Alex would put on his Robert Parker/Hawk act, "Brother, you don't want to know," and do a high-five.

They joked about going into the detective business together. There was an innocence about Alex, but an edginess as well.

Tracy said, "He tells Patti that he teaches computer science and literature courses online at the U. of Phoenix."

"That's absurd," Tom shook his head.

She continued, "When Patti challenged him, he told her to check Google. And she told him, 'But there's nothing here about Alex O'Reilly at the U. of Phoenix site.' So he told her to check Frank Edelweiss and James Altenheim. 'And that's you?' she asked. "He said of course and that he had a dozen other identities like Tom Cruise and Oprah Winfrey."

"He's just flirting with her," Tom explained.

"So lying is a turn-on?"

"Role play. *Mad About You*. You, of all people should understand that."

Around the house, Alex was a model housemate, always cleaning up after himself, and cooking bizarre dishes he invented on the fly, some of which were tasty.

In particular, Tom grew to like his odd-shaped Bisquick pizza, with a raisin sauce similar to his spaghetti sauce.

And Alex made time to walk with Patti to and from school each day.

He also got Patti into the advanced courses she wanted. And to celebrate that occasion, he had a t-shirt made for her that read, *Beware of the Ice Maiden*. In return, she gave him one of hers marked, *I'd rather be waring*.

Her creative writing course with Ms. Adams was more difficult than she had imagined. She had to write one page a day about anything for her journal. In addition, in two weeks she had to write and deliver orally a first-person monologue from the perspective of an everyday person who lived at least a hundred years ago.

She was stumped for a subject. "What relevance could anything from back then have to my life now?" she asked Marge rhetorically.

"Have you ever studied history?" Marge asked back.

"Of course. Right now I'm taking an upper level seminar on the Cold War."

"The Cold War? To me, that's not history; that's Current Events."

Patti explained, "The world today is totally different from a hundred years ago. Everything changes so fast. We face greater challenges today than any generation ever faced before, because of the accelerating rate of change. We need to focus on what's happening now and prepare for the future."

Marge laughed and shook her head, giving up on her.

Tracy suggested that Patti phone her grandparents. They could tell her things that they heard as kids about what it was like living around 1900—the kinds of things not found in books.

But Patti said, "No way." On her birth-mother's side, her grandparents died before she was born. And on her birth-father's side, they lived in Colorado. She'd only seen them twice. They were strangers. There was no way she could interview them over the phone.

Tom suggested, "Try my great-grandma Prudence. Just check the old photos and diaries in the attic."

"That's your attic, your past, your family."

"Make it yours, too."

"How could anybody with a name like Prudence be interesting?"

"Back in the 1870s, she probably sounded like you. Legend has it that she wouldn't back down to anybody. She ruled that clan of hers with a firm hand—all twelve kids."

"So she had spunk. She probably needed it to raise twelve kids. Three cheers for the Earth Mother. But how can I identify with someone who would have twelve children? It's just too weird, like someone from another planet."

"Well, she wasn't your typical Victorian lady. She ran away from home at fourteen and went by stagecoach to San Francisco. When she returned home five years later, her parents had told everyone that she had been visiting relatives in Ohio. Pru went along with that story and married a traditional man and had her twelve children. It wasn't until her parents and her husband had died that she started telling her grandchildren tales of her trip out West.

"There's a photo up in the attic of Pru walking up Commonwealth Avenue, parasol in hand, with all her progeny in their Sunday best, marching obediently behind her—like that kid's book *Make Way for Ducklings*. She was quite the matriarch. She commanded respect, which was why dozens of her neighbors joined her when she became a suffragette, and some of them even went to jail with her for demonstrating to get the vote for women.

"Then life threw her one curve ball after another. Her oldest son died in World War I, and her husband died in the influenza epidemic after the war, and her dead son's wife died of pneumonia. So she became a traditional mother again, this time raising her orphan grandson, my father, as if he were her own child. She supported her new family by working two jobs, as a free-lance reporter for the *Christian Science Monitor* and as a secretary at Emerson College."

Tom continued, "She was alert and active all through the Depression and World War II. When she was a hundred years old, I remember her playing blocks with me and trying to teach me the alphabet. You could say she was a serial mother—caring for three generations of kids."

"Amazing," noted Tracy.

"How could she stand it?" asked Patti, still belligerent.

"Spoken like someone who has never had children," answered Tom

"I'm with Patti on that one," Marge added.

"Okay," said Patti. "Say I decide to write about Pru. How am I supposed to get inside her mind. That's what the teacher wants—a first-person monologue. Sure, I could dig up some facts about her, but I still won't know how she thought."

"Read about nineteenth-century women's issues," Tracy suggested. "Check photos of Boston when Back Bay was new. Try to imagine what your life would have been like right here, back then."

"Yeah. I can imagine how depressed I'd be—no iPod, no cellphone, no computer, no television, no movies, no life to speak of."

Tracy coached her, "Start with the late 1860s, when Pru went out West. The Civil War had ended a few years before. The city streets were crowded with veterans, some still wearing pieces of their uniforms. Many were missing hands or arms or legs. Idealistic rebellious boys had come back as sober old men and reliable workers, trained to obey orders in factories and at construction sites. Business was thriving with these workers and their new families and young children. Demand was high for more housing and household products, in a world focused on material wealth."

"You should write this paper," Patti quipped.

Tracy continued, going full-speed ahead in teacher mode, "When you read, try to find a handle you can grab hold of—like the notion that the world that everyone had taken for granted for generations was ending."

"The times they were a changing."

"Indeed. They were then, and they are today," Tracy expounded. "Remember all those stories about the wild west—stagecoaches and Indians—"

"Native Americans."

"You know what happened in 1869, a few months after Pru set out?" asked Tracy.

"Some shootout in Deadwood?"

"The Transcontinental Railway. In May 1869 the last spike was driven in, joining the Union Pacific and the Central Pacific Railroads."

"Big deal."

"Very big," Tracy insisted. "Suddenly, you could go coast-to-coast by train in just a few days. Stagecoaches went out of business. The Pony Express went out of business. The Wild West was doomed. It would all be one happy smiling, suburban, homogenized workaday America. Pru must have seen it coming. Every day the newspapers reported on how fast the construction crews were moving. I imagine she ran away to see the wildness before it was gone forever."

"Like going whale watching or trying to spot a condor in the wilderness?"

"Exactly, run fast to see what you can before it's gone."

Taking Tracy's advice, Patti googled her way to hundreds of sites and read up on the temperance and suffrage movements. Online she found and read "Are Women People?" poems by Alice Duer Miller, "What Eight Million People Want" by Rhetta Childe Dorr, "Herland" by Charlotte Gilman, and "A Vindication of the Rights of Women" by Mary Wollstonecraft. She decided to take a Women's Studies course second semester. She stared at photos of offices back when typewriters had just been invented, and when it took pioneering courage for women to do clerical work, taking the jobs of the Bob Cratchits and Bartlebys of that day.

She was proud of the historically accurate, fact-filled paper she wrote for her creative writing class.

Ms. Adams, her teacher thought differently. "I didn't ask for an encyclopedia entry. Get inside your character.. Take as long as you need but get it right. You have a faraway look, like you have no idea what I'm talking about, but your Pru would have understood me. She would have read Bergson, her contemporary, who believed that the only path to truth is intuition. She would have read William James and heard him lecture. She might even have known him socially. He coined the phrase 'stream of consciousness.' Give me a monologue that makes me believe that you are her, living back then. If you can do that, then maybe you'll be able to give your readers a sense of what it's like to be you, here and now."

Despite Alex's encouragement and all the ideas he came up with as they walked back from BU that day, Patti was in tears by the time she got home.

"Check out the old clothes in the attic," Tracy suggested.

"Walk a mile in her shoes?"

"Well, maybe not the shoes, but everything else. You're into fashion. You understand the importance of a *look*. Dressing differently makes you feel differently. Dress like her to think like her."

"I can so imagine you in a corset," laughed Alex.

"No way," Patti countered. "I've seen *Pirates of the Caribbean*. I know that 'pain' and 'corset' are synonyms."

"No need for that," Tom interjected. "You won't find any corsets in the attic. Family legend has it that despite the styles of the day, Pru refused to wear such things. She dressed for comfort and personal pride. She liked to look good—but her own idea of good. She dressed for herself."

From the patterns in the trunk and the dressmaker's dummy that Alex fetched from the hidden room, it looked like Pru designed and made her own clothes. The waist was a normal waist, not meant to be pulled in tight, and the long skirts hung evenly down to below the ankles. The tops were designed for a full bust, like Patti's.

Many items had deteriorated beyond repair. But Patti found five dresses with matching hats and parasols, which could be salvaged. They were all solid colors: red, green, blue, violet, and black.

Patti brought the dressmaker's dummy down from the attic. It was close to her size and remarkably lifelike—not just a torso—almost a complete wood and plaster-of-paris statue. She made minor adjustments with the screws, using her own clothes as a template and used the dummy to make alterations in Pru's clothes so they fit her better.

Then she took those dresses, hats and parasols to a tailor shop on Newbury Street and had them repaired and dyed to restore their original look.

For several days in a row, when she got home from school, she tried on one outfit or another, modeling in front of the full-length mirror on her door.

Finally, she wore the violet outfit to class, with her usual sneakers, so she could walk normally. There was no way she could manage in the clodhoppers from the trunk.

All day she kept a straight face despite the bewildered stares she drew from teachers and fellow students.

Ms. Adams simply smiled and nodded.

Three more days of living her daily life in Pru's clothes made Patti ready to write her next draft.

"You're getting warmer," Ms. Adams noted. "You show me what she would look like to others walking up Commonwealth Avenue, and how she herself would feel. But what would she think? Imagine that you are

Pru, and you are taking this course back then, and your assignment is to write a monologue from the perspective of someone named Patti living a hundred years in the future. You know all the facts, but you need to, with words, help your contemporaries experience what it would be like to live at that future time—now."

"No way," Patti insisted. "That sounds like something out of *The Terminator* or *Back to the Future* with past and future getting all mixed up in impossible ways."

"Just think logically. Compare Patti's world and Pru's world. Someone today has to learn how to use one new video game system after another. But to someone back then, electric light is new. You had to learn how to use cell phones. To Pru, the telephone itself is new. You have to move from one generation of sound and video recording to another. To Pru the concept of recording anything is new and revolutionary. Today movies come out with advanced new special effects. To Pru silent movies were new and magical. Today more fuel-efficient cars and planes are developed. Pru, in her lifetime, saw the very first cars and planes. You can vote, but probably haven't bothered to yet. Pru devoted her life to winning for women legal equality and the right to vote.

"Perspective gives life to a story—whatever the time and setting. It can make the ordinary seem magical. Tolstoy wrote a story from the perspective of a horse. Be grateful I didn't give you that as an assignment. Try writing from Pru's perspective in the late nineteenth century."

Alex suggested total immersion—spending a weekend living in the attic, reading Pru's old diaries, with no distractions, like in Jack Finney's time travel novel *Time and Again*.

"But the burglars," Patti objected.

"I'll take care of them," he winked. "I have connections. No one will bother you."

Patti didn't know whether to feel reassured or disconcerted to think that Alex might have some connection with the burglars.

"Take all the food and drink you'll need and don't take a cell phone," Alex ordered. "You can come down to use the bathroom, but shut your eyes when you do," he joked.

After an hour of reading Pru's diaries on Friday night, Patti came down to get Tylenol. "It's absolutely impossible," she complained to

Tracy and Alex. "The diaries just record the weather and the children's health. There are endless pages of shopping lists. Those diaries give no sense of what kind of person Pru was, and what she thought and cared about, and what it was like to live at that time. I feel like one of the archaeologists who deciphered that mysterious old Greek language."

"Linear B," Tracy told her, "Mycenean. Far older than ancient Greek."

"Well, the way I understand it," Patti continued, "they had stacks of texts which everybody thought might give insight into a lost period of history and literature. But when they'd figured the language out, they realized that all that writing was just inventory lists. Well, that's how I feel about those diaries. This whole project is a bust. There's no way I can pass this course. And now it's too late to switch back to freshman English. I am so totally screwed."

"Immersion, remember, like Alex said—immersion," Tracy coached her. "It doesn't matter what Pru wrote. It's like putting on those old clothes—only you're doing it to your mind. Make your eyes read the words that she wrote while you sit in a place where she sat, surrounded with stuff that was hers. The ideas will come to you."

Since she had nothing better to do, she went back up the ladder.

That was when she stumbled upon the real story of Pru's life.

13 ~ Pru's Diaries

That Sunday morning, Patti opened a diary that looked like the others, and a derringer pistol dropped out. The front pages had been cut in the shape of the gun to conceal it. Text was written on the back pages.

No weather. No children's health. No shopping lists. Instead, Patti found an account of violent death, a story that Pru, apparently, had never told anyone.

Pru didn't say what she did with the body. Considering her frame of mind when she wrote this, she may not have remembered what she did with it.

Patti read that account repeatedly. Then she went down to Alex's room. She shut the door and hushed him to prevent him from asking questions that might interrupt the flow of her thoughts. Then she performed the story for him, in the first person.

***

I killed a man.

I have twelve children.

No one knows.

Every Sunday afternoon, my husband and I and our twelve children, dressed in their finest, walk down the park in the middle of Commonwealth Avenue, all the way from Fairfield Street to the Boston Common and back.

No one knows.

At fourteen, I ran away from home and went to California, alone by stagecoach.

No one knows.

He presumed I was helpless.

The doorbell rang.

My husband, Nate, was out. We had just moved into this new house. Nate would be interviewing tenants and serered servants this coming weekend. Our friends and relatives knew that we had just moved in and needed time to settle. All alone, I was playing the role of proper Boston matron, reading the morning paper and sipping tea, imagining I would soon invite our new neighbors over and we would talk about the next fundraiser for the Museum of Fine Arts, or discuss the latest lecture by William James, or the latest novel by his brother Henry. I was a little girl, pretending to be a grownup.

Who could be at the door?

The "gas man" he said.

But the gas had been hooked up last week. The gas lights and gas stove worked just fine.

I was alone. There was no reason for me to be disturbed by some stranger.

When I was in Frisco I held a derringer for the first time.

A leak had been reported in the neighborhood, this man said. He needed to inspect. It would be quick and painless, he said through the mail slot.

I opened the door a crack, and he forced it open the rest of the way, grabbing me and spinning me around, and putting a knife to my throat before I could scream.

I took quick shallow breaths. The blade was scratching my skin. I could feel a drop of blood forming.

If he spoke, I didn't hear the words.

After five years, I had returned from the west, as if that episode of my life had never happened. Mom and Dad had told everyone that I'd been visiting my Aunt Mim and Uncle Hank in Ohio.

Maybe I never ran away. The dust, the heat, the drunken groping hands, the scratches, the knife wounds, even the sound of seals barking at dawn in the harbor, that I remembered—maybe all that had happened to someone else. It was a story I had once heard.

At twenty-two, I was mistress of a fine new house in Back Bay, married to a professor of philosophy, a veteran of the Civil War.

My present was comfortable. My future was secure. The past didn't matter.

I believed in God and in my husband. I did not need to believe in myself. Everything would be taken care of for me. I would be respected by all, protected by all, and I would have the leisure and the wealth to enjoy literature and art, and the society of other refined, educated clever people.

That knife at my throat ended that illusion.

I was meat to be cut, then left to rot.

He smelled of whisky and rancid sweat.

He forced me to walk upstairs to my apartment.

In the kitchen, my cup of tea was still on the table, with a half-eaten biscuit. Nate's top-hat hung from a post on the wall.

With his left hand, he ripped my blouse open and grasped a breast, pinching the nipple; the knife was ready to slice my windpipe if I tried to yell.

This was not me. This could not be me. This could not happen to me in my own house in Boston in the nineteenth century.

He moved with confidence, guiding me where he wanted to go. He had done this before and was operating by habit. Otherwise he would have done whatever he was going to do on the stairs or in the kitchen or in a bedroom. Instead, still keeping the knife to my throat, with his left hand he grabbed the pole and opened the trap door to the attic, pulled down the ladder, and forced me to go up.

He was familiar with the layout of the house—identical to others on the block. Why had I not heard that neighbors had been attacked? Were they so afraid of scandal that they'd leave others unwarned and unprepared? Were they afraid to tell their husbands, much less the police?

Reaching the attic, I tried to slam the trapdoor shut on his head, but he anticipated that move and countered with the pole.

As I spun away to the right, toward the window, his knife grazed my right calf.

I reached the window, threw it open, climbed out onto the walkway, then slammed it shut and held it down with my full weight until my strength gave out. He didn't need to break the window. He could simply overpower me—and he seemed proud to demonstrate that.

I ran along the walkway, with the "gas man" at my heels.

I flung open the window to the "hiding place"—a secret room that Nate had said would always be the safest room in the house.

I climbed in but couldn't pull the window shut before he grabbed it from below and forced it up.

I fell back, toppling over boxes of my private things—relics from my past that no one knew of but me.

Looking back over my shoulder, all I could see was a beam of sunlight, partly blocked by his shadow, which moved slowly, confidently toward where I cowered in the corner, behind a stack of boxes, as if I could hide in an 8 x 12 space, as if I could use cardboard to defend myself.

I heard ripping cloth before I felt him tug again and again, tearing off my skirt and petticoats.

I could see the blade swing back and forth, passing within an inch of my bare legs.

I crouched, making myself small, imagining that I was a kitten, a sparrow, an ant—small enough to hide in this debris.

Then my mind and body separated.

My mind was already in a coffin. I was ready to go toward the bright light on the other side of his shadow.

But my body squirmed, and my hands scrambled, feeling their way along the floor, identifying pieces of my past that had tumbled around me—boots, belts, kerchiefs.

The shadow moved slowly, as if he drew pleasure from control, from watching me cower and squirm, from depriving me of all dignity, making me his plaything. Toying with me, he swung the knife like a pendulum, ever so close to my now bare belly.

My left hand touched silk, and I saw images from the day I bought that red scarf from a Chinese matron on a wharf in Frisco. I heard the barking of seals in the harbor, as I bought something else from that old lady—something small but deadly.

I had never used it except for practice—hours of practice, for the confidence it gave me. In the old days, I had always kept it loaded.

My right hand chanced upon the familiar shape.

My mind rushed back from the shadow and the light.

After two years, there might not be a bullet in the chamber. I might not be able to shoot accurately.

Maybe I should do nothing at all.

He might just humiliate me to assert his power, and then leave.

He might just use my body, and then leave.

He might just hurt me for the pleasure of hurting me, and then leave.

If the gun misfired or I missed, he would surely torture and kill me.

I don't remember the shot.

I told no one.

I just wanted to forget.

I wanted to forget. I wanted my life to go on as if this had never happened. And on the surface, my life did go on undisturbed—like on Sunday afternoons with Nate and our children marching proudly down Commonwealth Avenue.

But I was far less patient with fools, far less willing to put up with behavior and laws that went counter to my sense of fairness or justice. I will stand up for what I believe, against the will of anyone.

I remember very little from the moment of the shot until the birth of my first son.

That was when I bought this silver chain that fits tightly around my throat, covering the scar from his knife blade. I have worn it every day since then, a reminder of the blade—the narrow edge that separates life from death.

***

Alex applauded. "Congratulations. You did a great job on that tricky assignment."

"No, that was just an improv. I haven't written anything yet."

"Then do it again, and I'll take it down as dictation on my laptop.

She performed it twice, and he captured it all.

Then she performed it for him once again, simply because she needed to, like a marathoner jogging an extra quarter mile to unwind.

14 ~ In Search of Alex

Patti did another performance for Marge, Tom, and Tracy. Tom and Marge applauded, but Tracy was spooked, and it had spooked Patti to realize that someone posing as a gas man had tried to murder someone in this house and had been shot to death and the body left to rot in the attic.

Tom reassured them, "Claiming to be a gas man is a common routine to get in the front door. That's why we were upset that you fell for it. As coincidences go, I'm not surprised by that one. Does the missing body bother you? Hey, she got rid of it. That's all that matters. Three generations of kids played up there—me included—day after day, and nothing bad happened. You aren't trapped in some B-grade movie. A skeleton isn't going to fall on you up there. There are no ghosts. There's no danger from back then."

"Hug me." Tracy asked him.

"Gladly."

Patti turned to Alex, "Is there anything you can do to make the fear go away?"

"Let's make a scare-ghost," he suggested.

"A what?"

"A scarecrow for ghosts."

They put Pru's violet outfit on the dressmaker's model and carried it up to the hiding room.

"Does that do it?" asked Alex.

"And what will the burglars think of it?" asked Tom.

"I think they've already moved on."

"And what makes you think that?"

"Connections."

"You and your connections," complained Patti.

"Well, you haven't heard any noises up here lately, have you? And you've been up here a lot, Patti. If and when they come back to collect their stuff, seeing the dummy dressed up like this they'll know that we've been here and guess that we know that they've been using the place. So they'll clear out quick and leave us alone."

"If it's that easy to get rid of them, why didn't we do it before?" asked Tom.

"It didn't occur to me until now," Alex admitted.

"And what about the gun?" Patti handed him the derringer. "Do you think it might still work?"

"I'll check it out. I've got friends. I'll get it fixed if it needs fixing. Then hide it on our scare-ghost here. That should give it more cosmic power," he joked.

Within a few days, the derringer was cleaned and oiled and Alex bought ammunition for it. He put it in the pocket of the violet dress on the "scare-ghost" and told Patti mockingly, "Now if anyone attacks you up here, you'll be ready."

"You seem to know a lot about guns."

"They call me Quick Draw O'Reilly."

***

Tracy bombarded Tom with speculations about Alex and his shady connections. "Alex says he's wanted by the Feds for computer hacking or viruses or something like that," she told Tom. "I think he makes up outrageous stories about himself as a way to show off and flirt. But it's unnerving that one or more of those stories might be true."

Another time she told Tom that Alex had told her he had started college but dropped out when accused of stealing laptops.

"Did he clear his name?"

"No. He skipped town and changed his name and went into hiding."

"But he was innocent, of course?"

"Technically, yes. He never stole a thing, he says. But he told others what to steal and how to do it. And he fenced the stuff online. He claims he got orders for machines with particular specs before the fact, and juggled parts and installed software to satisfy what the customers wanted."

Tom laughed. "The kid has an imagination. And did this tale turn you on?"

"Well, maybe a little."

"But you didn't do anything about it?"

"Of course not, Tom. He's just a kid."

"Next he's going to tell you he's a secret agent. Sounds like *True Lies*."

"Okay, so I'm a sucker for drama. Give me some."

"Some what?"

"Drama. Break out of the routine we've slipped into. You have a spooky attic, with trunks of old clothes. Role play. You're the one who likes that *Mad About You* shtick. Let's do it."

"But just a week ago, the thought of the attic made you too scared to sleep."

"That was a week ago. Besides, remember, Alex guaranteed to Patti that nobody would disturb her up there. He knows something. It's really safe. But the thought there might be danger, could be one hell of a turn on."

So after the others had gone to their rooms and shut their lights out, Tom and Tracy quietly went up the ladder to the attic. There Tracy put on a show, dressing up in long skirts without tops, and then in blouses with nothing else on.

"I'm thinking about getting a tongue stud," she teased him.

"Gross," he reacted.

"Hey, consider the possibility." She stuck her tongue out and wiggled it. "Imagine what I could do with it. Whether I do it or don't do it, just imagine that I'm the kind of person who might do it."

Suddenly, they heard footsteps and muffled voices. As a reflex, they dropped to the floor. Then they looked through the trap door. The kitchen was empty. The noises were coming from the hidden room.

They went down the ladder quickly and quietly, let the ladder up, and bolted the trap door shut.

"Now do you believe that Alex isn't in cahoots with the burglars?" Tom whispered.

"Yes and no," Tracy speculated. "He found my Kindle too fast. And he gave us clues where to look for that silver stuff of yours and my laptop. And he was too confident when he told Patti to stay up there alone for an entire weekend. And now the burglars are back. So either he knew about their movements in advance, or he ordered them to stay away temporarily. Either way he's messing with the dark side."

In the morning, Marge mentioned she had heard squirrels in the attic again.

"Yes, it probably was squirrels this time," Alex affirmed.

Before Tom had a chance to contradict him and challenge him with Tracy's latest speculations, Alex offered Tom some freelance software work. He asked Tom to write Web software on contract for some friends of his who were involved in a joint venture. They could pay him nearly $5000 for a job that would probably take him just three or four days. Each of ten partners would pay him $499—half in advance, half on completion. That way they wouldn't have to file 1099s, for miscellaneous payments for contract work. Tom could report the income. All above board. But they'd have less paperwork hassle.

"What kind of software?" Tom asked, sitting down for a serious conversation.

"Your kind. Of course I googled you. It's the same kind of work you did before you were laid off. In fact, my sources tell me you're one of the best. It's for a web-based business. There would be several separate pieces. Collecting fees for club membership and keeping track of members and matching them randomly with one another while maintaining anonymity. Just sign a standard non-disclosure agreement, and I'll give you the details you need to get started."

"So this is what you've been up to, Alex?"

"Sure, Web-based business, partnering, and online auctions stuff, like the advice I gave to Patti's dad."

"And your secrecy?" Tom insisted.

"You know what it's like with startups these days. You can never be too careful, especially with a good idea that's easy to implement. A few stray words repeated innocently in an email, and a competitor hits the market with the same kind of thing before you do."

"A little paranoid, perhaps?"

"The vertigo of online business," Alex concluded.

***

"Business?" Tracy exploded when Tom told her. "Legitimate business? Don't be ridiculous. This has something to do with his gang of burglars. Don't get involved."

"But I am involved. I'm working on the project already."

"But if this company you are working for is a criminal enterprise—"

"Tracy, this is just contract work. I'm a freelancer. I'm responsible for writing code, period. It's standard business practice to wall off contractors from the strategic business plan—a matter of confidentiality. What I don't need to know to do the work, they don't tell me. And as long as I don't know, what the company does with it isn't my worry. Besides, I have no reason to doubt this is legitimate. Alex is a great guy. And the software is standard stuff, with a few harmless twists. Let's drop the Alex-phobia. Think more about me and less about him. So when are you going to get that tongue stud?"

"And when are you going to get one, too?"

"Ouch!"

15 ~ A Walk on the Dark Side

Meanwhile Tom started sampling Italian restaurants and took a two-week course in Italian cooking at Boston Adult Education. His father had died of diabetes. For the last thirty years of his life his father had had to monitor his glucose, and give himself insulin injections, and couldn't eat pasta or any other high-carb foods that he loved. Tom wanted to enjoy good food while he still could, but Tracy avoided restaurants and bars in her off hours. For her, eating at home was a welcome change of pace.

So Tracy didn't come along when Tom took Alex to a three-star Italian restaurant in the North End to celebrate completion of and payment for the software.

For the occasion, Alex wore sunglasses and a 1930's suit jacket and tie that Patti had uncovered in the attic. He explained with a grin, "When in Mob Land, dress like mobsters do." On the way there, he drew stares from everyone, even exotically clad young ladies with blue and green wigs.

"Now Tomaso," Alex began to explain in a Hollywood Sicilian accent, "I didn't want to do this, but my partners insist."

"Sure, Guido, sure."

"You see that software you wrote was for a nationwide drop-ship network."

"That much I could guess from the specs."

"And this network was set up to fence stolen goods by way of eBay."

"Now that's rich, Alex — I mean Guido. With ties to the Back Bay attic burglars, no doubt. You could almost have me believe that."

Alex kept a poker face and a consistent accent. "Burglary is a high-risk business because you wind up with goods that you have to fence. That means that for each burglary there are three risky operations you've got to go through — stealing the goods, transferring the goods to a fence, and then the fence selling the goods. And all these operations typically take place in the same city, so if cops uncover hot merchandise on the street, they can follow the trail back to you.

"In addition, the retail marketplace stinks. TVs and computers used to be our best items. But nowadays discount wholesalers sell new TVs and computers for less than we used to get for second-hand. And the manufacturers keep coming out with new models that make the old ones obsolete. So we need to find buyers quick, or the merchandise will be worth nothing. And even when we do find buyers, margins are low."

"Great spiel, Alex," said Tom, taking a big forkful of spaghetti. "And great advice too—I'll be sure not to buy stock in burglary companies."

"So along comes the Internet and on-line auctions, and techy fences start to post their wares on eBay; which works okay for a while, until the cops wake up and start doing searches for hot goods on eBay. Sure they don't catch everybody, but a few collars and word gets around and the average fence gets spooked. Besides, it's a lot of time and trouble taking photos, writing descriptions, and posting the items for sale—and that's not the kind of work your average fence is good at. And typically, they don't know enough about the Internet to mask their own identity and the origin of the goods."

"Okay, Guido, okay. Enough. And do you think the Sox can win the series again this year?"

"That's where you come in."

"The Sox?"

"No, Tomaso. The dropship network."

"Now you're starting to scare me."

"Good. That means you're listening. I don't want to have to repeat myself."

"What kind of game is this, Alex?"

"It's a variation on the old shell game—matching buyers and sellers anonymously, so the buyers have no idea where the hot merchandise came from. The drop-ship club is members only. The burglar provides the description and photo for each item—following on-line advice available only to members. He submits the listing to the club, where it gets randomly assigned to a drop-ship member. Then he ships the goods to that guy, with no return address. The burglar remains anonymous. The drop-ship member offers the item to legitimate eBay retailers who are looking for merchandise to sell. The retailer posts the item as an auction at eBay. When someone wins that auction, the retailer notifies the drop shipper, who sends it straight to the end customer. No one knows where the goods came from—not the customer, not the drop-shipper, not the eBay merchant. We take the risk out of the burglary business."

"Sounds like a good tagline for your television ads. But why are you telling me this? Why do you need to show off how clever you are?"

"You did a great job, Tomaso. My partners are so impressed that they want to bring you into the operation."

"Stop right there. I don't want to hear any more. Whether this is a sick joke or serious business, I don't want anything to do with it."

"But my friends, Tomaso, they want you. They'd like you to run the technical side of the operation, and they're willing to pay big bucks for your services."

"This is ridiculous," Tom stood up and started to walk away.

"Not so fast, Tomaso. You are already implicated."

"All I did was write some software on contract."

"But now you know what that software was for. That makes you an accomplice. And don't expect to go to the police. Just imagine their reaction if you repeat this wild story that you heard from a college-age kid in a mock 1930's costume in an Italian restaurant in the North End. It could all be a put-on, a practical joke that was misunderstood. And if someone believed it was real, you share an apartment with the guy, and what cop is going to believe you didn't know what the software was about in the first place? Sit down. Calm down. And listen."

"How could you do this to me? I trusted you. We're friends."

"So wake up and listen," Alex dropped the accent. "You are far too trusting. When I came to your door, hoping to rent the room, it wasn't for the WiFi connection, it was because of the hidden room. The attic burglars had found it and wanted to use it for temporary storage, but they wanted some assurance that it wouldn't be messed with. They asked me to do what I could as a favor—nothing illegal—and I deal in favors, and you made it far too easy for me."

"So you were one of them from the start?"

"Not so simple, Tom. I have friends, Tom, lots of friends. Some of them happen to be in the burglary business. I do favors for them. They do favors for me. And they were enthusiastic about this Web-based business idea I came up with late one night, over beers."

"Tell me I can wake up now. Tell me that this was a nightmare."

"Okay, Tom, you can wake up now. It's over. I'm done with it, and so you're done with it. I was in way over my head, and I couldn't hold my breath much longer. The big bucks were tempting, but I've ended it."

"What?"

"The burglars cleared the stuff out of the attic last night, and they won't be back."

"And the drop-ship network?"

"It hasn't been launched yet, and if and when it ever is, it won't be with me."

"But how?"

"Locally, it's just an exchange of favors—now I owe the burglars instead of them owing me. Globally, it was all laid out in the original agreement. Never start any business without establishing an exit strategy. I paid some serious money to the Web partners as an early termination fee."

"I don't like that word."

"What word?"

"Termination."

"Don't worry. Aside from the fee, which is only fair, considering what my backing out will cost them, I'm well protected. It's an Internet-style Mexican standoff—like the old global nuclear strategy: mutually assured destruction."

"I don't know what to say."

"Try thank you. And remember, you owe me one."

"One what."

"One humongous favor."

Tom stared in disbelief.

16 ~ Not Exactly Brothers and Sisters

As Tom learned later that while he and Alex were at dinner Tracy got a tongue stud.

When Tracy got home, Patti noticed immediately and was fascinated, "Wow! Did it hurt?"

"A little more than having your ears pierced. A lot less than a trip to the dentist."

"And what's it feel like?"

"Like having a stranger's tongue in my mouth."

"And guys like it?"

"We'll soon find out."

"What did Tom say?"

"It's a surprise."

"And you think he'll want to feel that—"

"All over him."

She took Patti's hand and ran her newly equipped tongue slowly from fingertips to elbow.

"Double wow."

Tracy put her hands behind Patti's head and drew her near until their lips almost touched, then gave a quick flick of her tongue to Patti's upper lip and pulled back.

"Think about it. That's what you have to do with a guy—make him think about it. Sex is 90% in the mind. As soon as he sees this, the anticipation will start, and regardless of whether my tongue ever touches him, he'll be mine to do with as I please."

"And you know that even though you've never tried it?"

"I know men."

"Do you think that would turn Alex on?"

"Well, I'm not interested in Alex," Tracy insisted.

"No, I didn't mean you and Alex. I meant do you think Alex would be interested in me that way if I had one of those?"

"Alex is already interested in you. Why do you think he goes back and forth to school with you every day? Why do you think he has such trouble looking you in the eyes?"

"I think he's a virgin."

"What?"

"I think that's why. I think he hasn't had much experience with girls. And the way I dress, I think he has the wrong idea about me. I mean like I've only really done it with one guy—and that was in France last summer."

"Well, if that's the case, if he ever gets over his fear of rejection, he'll be all over you. So don't play coy, let him know you want him."

"But I thought that would scare him away."

"You've watched too many old movies. This isn't the 1930s. Make the first move. If I'd waited for Tom to speak up, we'd have gone no further than barroom flirtation."

"Thanks, Tracy. You're great. I never had a big sister to explain things like that to me."

***

When he got home, Tom was still distracted by what he had heard from Alex. That was all he could talk to Tracy about. He didn't notice Tracy's tongue stud.

She made a point of opening her mouth wide, but still he didn't notice.

She kissed him and inserted her tongue, and still he didn't notice.

So she picked up her Kindle and read a J.D. Robb novel while Tom droned on about Alex.

Meanwhile, Alex confessed to Patti what he had told Tom. The burglars were in the attic because of him. Thanks to him, Tom was implicated in a large-scale criminal enterprise. Now he had broken off all ties with the bad guys, and he was begging her for forgiveness, as if he expected her to say that none of this mattered and to take him in her arms and comfort him.

Patti was shocked. Yes, she had played with the notion that Alex had a dark side and an evil past, as if she were experimenting with plots for stories. But this man she had felt drawn to was a liar and a criminal.

Still dressed in his outlandish 1930s garb, his repentance came across as a theatrical act. And if she kept peeling the layers of the onion, would there ever be a real Alex inside, or whatever his real name was?

She backed away, then dashed into her room and slammed the door, and pushed her bureau against the door, as if that would provide more protection. Then she sank to the floor and sobbed.

***

After Tom fell asleep, Tracy went to the kitchen for chips to snack on and found Alex at his laptop at the kitchen table.

She flashed her tongue stud and he noticed immediately.

On impulse, she asked, "Want to taste?"

He nodded.

From Tom's ramblings, she knew that Alex was creatively wicked. She also knew that the burglars had cleared out of the attic, never to return.

She unbolted the trap door, pulled down the ladder, and led Alex up to the attic.

***

Marge heard noises coming from the attic and knocked on Tom's door. "Good God!" she told him. "Am I the only one who hears them? They're back again."

"Who?"

"The burglars. And don't tell me you don't hear them."

"But Alex said—"

"And when are you going to stop believing him, and start protecting us?" She marched over to the trap door and slammed the lock shut.

That was when Tom realized that Tracy wasn't in his room and wasn't in the kitchen.

He knocked on Alex's door. When there was no answer, he opened it. No one was there.

He knocked on Patti's door. After a long pause, she pushed the bureau aside and opened the door. No, she had no idea where Tracy and Alex were.

The noises from the attic grew louder. Tom, Marge, and Patti sat at the kitchen table and stared at the trap door in bewilderment.

At dawn, Tom went for a long walk. He wasn't home when Marge, before leaving for work, finally unlocked the trap door and let them down. Patti left for school alone.

When Tom got back, Tracy was gone, and Alex was in a deep sleep.

Tracy didn't come home that night.

The following morning, Tom called her on her cell.

She answered immediately.

She was boarding a plane to San Francisco. "Meeghan says it's great out there," she explained.

She said that she had intended to call once she arrived. She didn't want to risk being talked out of her decision.

***

Alex told Tom, "So now I owe you big time, instead of you owing me."

Tom stared up at the attic, then replied, "I'm not sure about that. It's going to take a while to sort this out. Right now it hurts too much to tell. But in the long run, I just might end up thanking you."

17 ~ A Good Job Was Had by All

The next morning, as Marge was getting ready for work and Patti was about to leave for school, alone, the phone rang.

"They're back," moaned Patti, in imitation of the line from the *Poltergeist* movie.

After the second ring, Marge picked it up, listened, then shouted, "Alex, it's for you."

"Hang it up," he yelled, stumbling out of his room, apparently having slept in his clothes. "Hang it up now!"

She did.

"Caller ID?" he asked.

"Private number."

"The voice?" he asked.

"It sounded like a guy your age. It wasn't the same person as before. I'm sure of that."

"No one that I know has that number," Alex insisted.

"On the contrary," Tom added, as he joined the others in the kitchen. "Apparently someone does."

"Okay, what can we do?" Marge asked.

Alex suggested, "We could put anonymous call blocker on the line — but that would only help with local calls from unlisted numbers. Calls from outside this area code or from a cell phone or made with a phone card would all still come through as a private number."

"We could call the police, and Tom's phone company," suggested Marge. "Then whenever a suspicious call comes in we could do a star-57 and the call would be traced."

Alex shook his head. "Calls made with phone cards and prepaid cell phones can't be traced. And someone like this would definitely do it that way."

"Someone like what?" asked Marge.

"Someone trying to intimidate us."

"Why?"

"Maybe to get us to move out."

"Why?"

"I don't know."

"The police," insisted Marge. "Whether they can trace it or not, we should tell the police. There's no telling what kind of nutcase this guy is."

"No," Alex quickly added. "There's no need to bring in the cops. What would you tell them anyway? That we've had a few calls with different voices asking to talk to different people who live here? No threats. No obscenity. And the calls were made at reasonable hours. What's the crime?"

"I'll change the number," suggested Tom. "I'll have it unlisted. I'll only tell Diane and the kids. They're the only ones who call my landline anyway."

***

They soon fell into a new routine. Tom once again went to the gym each day, Marge to work, and Patti to school. After that last bizarre phone call, Alex hung out in the attic, presumably to be alone with his thoughts.

For supper, Tom and Alex alternated—Tom cooked Italian, and Alex came up with new hodgepodges, starting with Tom's leftovers.

After a week, Tom summoned the courage to apologize to Marge. "I should never have brought her here."

"And could you have told her no?"

"No."

"Then don't worry about it. It was no surprise. Tracy, like Alex, was thinking about her exit strategy from the beginning. I don't know what she said to you, but to me she dropped hints that she had a thing for younger men, that she thought you had a thing for me, and that the day shift wasn't her kind of life—not forever."

That night Marge saw Tom playing Sudoku and joined him on the sofa. He used to be addicted to that game but hadn't played since the arrival of Tracy. He hadn't played Free Cell either. Tracy didn't like games.

Tom and Marge did one Sudoku after another, working together. Their styles were different, but complementary. Tom might see at a glance that a particular number belonged in a particular square, and then would back-track to check and explain why. Marge would analyze all the possibilities, square by square, and number by number, until she had written down all the candidate numbers for every square. Then she would look for opportunities, by process of elimination—looking for instances where the number was clear, and then she would erase candidate numbers that were eliminated. Sometimes, Tom would come up with one or two numbers by intuition, and thanks to Marge's analysis, others would fall into place, and they would quickly finish the puzzle.

They played one after the other until they fell asleep next to one another.

Patti woke them in the morning, getting ready for school, and waved a mock-accusing finger at them, "So you're sleeping together already. And just a week after Tracy took off. I never would have expected that of you."

Tom blushed. Marge laughed.

That morning Alex walked Patti to school again, and Tom walked Marge to work, presumably as a safety measure. After work, Marge met him at Gold's Gym and bought a membership. She was already in the habit of regular exercise to erase the stresses of the office as well as to stay in shape. Now she did it in the gym instead of the privacy of her room. They then walked home together.

One afternoon on the way back from BU, on Commonwealth near the intersection with Massachusetts Avenue, first Alex, then Patti realized that someone was following them, keeping half a block behind. He was as tall as the gas man, but had a beard and wore a dark raincoat, despite the clear sky. He was either extremely stupid, or he deliberately wanted them to know that he was following them.

Patti assumed the man was after Alex. But Alex insisted that no one had it in for him now. He made her promise not to tell Marge and Tom. They would speculate wildly and worry, and that wouldn't help anyone.

Marge sensed something was wrong and prodded until she heard the whole story about the burglars and the online scheme and Alex being followed. "Alex, you're the one who needs protection," she concluded. "Whether it's legitimate business or monkey business, there are people who want to intimidate you. If you have to go out, don't go alone. And stay in public places, no loitering in dark alleys, do you hear me?"

But Alex continued to play guardian to Patti. The next day, he gave Patti a wireless headset in the form of earrings that connected to a cell phone she could keep in her pocket.

That same day a package arrived from Amazon—a Kindle that Alex had bought for Patti. He loaded it with 19th century novels, and she delighted in reading works she had never heard of before by Stevenson, Scott, and Kipling.

On Tuesday nights and some weekends, Alex disappeared, without explanation. Patti followed him one Tuesday and discovered that he was playing in tournaments at the Boylston Chess Club. She signed up for the same tournament and placed second, winning double her entry fee, while Alex finished out of the money. He didn't notice her until the last round, when they were paired against one another, and she beat him in a tricky rook-and-pawn endgame.

He showed no surprise at seeing her there, or at her beating him. Afterwards, he went over the moves with her, pointing out where she and he could have done better and citing classic games in which similar positions had occurred. She had never read a chess book and had never played in a tournament before. She had learned playing against her computer, gradually increasing the difficulty level.

The next Tuesday, they walked over to the Club together. And several times a week they played together in the attic where they wouldn't be interrupted.

In the past, Alex sometimes explained his global business dealings in terms of chess. What mattered wasn't just the pieces on the board, but their mobility and position, preparing for possible future moves. He saw the board in terms of energy and dynamic tension. You didn't always strive to make a deal or take a piece. Often the best move improved your position for making future moves, gave your pieces wider ranging play, improved your defense, or accentuated a weakness in the enemy's position. Often the best move attacked and defended at the same time, building the tension.

Now he explained chess strategy to Patti using examples from his business maneuvers. He gave her a quick tour of web sites of companies he had dealings with. She recognized this openness as a sign of his growing respect for her intelligence. And she found such treatment far more attractive than flirtatious flattery about her good looks.

Then with no explanation, for several days, Alex spent a lot of time alone in the attic. Patti walked to school alone and even went to the Boylston Chess Club alone.

At his request, she kept her cell phone connected to his all day long. She liked feeling that they were close even when apart.

When, out of curiosity, Patti checked on him in the attic, she found him in the hiding room, engrossed in comic books rather than on his laptop, as if, stressed out, he were regressing.

"What's with the comic books?" she asked.

"I'm just having fun in my own way. Nothing to worry about." He explained that his parents used to throw out his comic books and old toys when he "grew out of them." He was an only child. There was no need to save things for the next kid. Amidst all this old stuff in the attic, he was feeling nostalgic and thinking of building an eBay past.

"A what?" asked Patti.

"Many people who grew up like me pay ridiculous prices on eBay for old stuff, like these comics, trying to recapture childhood memories."

"That's strange," answered Patti. "I have all my old stuff. It's all stored in boxes I haven't opened in years. My parents—all my parents—were probably trying to make me feel comfortable and secure despite their shuffling and reshuffling the family with their divorces and marriages. I took it for granted that my stuff would always be saved. I never looked at it—except my first teddy bear, which sits in the bottom drawer of my bureau at home. It just feels good to know that the rest of my old stuff is safely stored in case I might want it someday.

"So you just come up here and read comic books?" she went on. "It has nothing to do with the gas man or the Mob chasing you?"

"Yes, comic books," he looked away, in no mood for confiding. "That's just me being me. Besides, there's something special about this place and its history."

"I used to have a recurrent dream," Patti confided, "about our house in Plymouth, New Hampshire. It has an attached barn, with a cupola and an unused attic. In the dream, there was a secret room on the other side of the attic wall. If I could just find my way in, the room held answers."

"But you didn't know the questions?"

"Of course not," she chuckled. "And just like *Hitch Hiker's Guide*, that would have been the stumper." Then she probed, hoping to catch him off guard, "Who are you running from and why?"

He picked up the comic books and put them back in their boxes, organized by series and date. Then, sitting Indian-style on the mattress on the floor, he leaned back against the dressmaker's model and told his tale.

"You're right. Somebody's probably after me. I don't know who. Hundreds of people have lost jobs or money because of deals I've made."

He looked weary. She took his hand in hers, and petted it gently, like she would a hurt kitten. Finally he looked her in the eye, unguarded — like Jack Sparrow pulling off a full-face mask to reveal a frightened teenage kid. She took his head in her hands so he wouldn't look away. Their noses touched.

Afterwards, she didn't know if they kissed at all that first time. Everything happened quickly, without words. Then they did it twice more, slowly, with kisses, and fell asleep together.

When they woke in a beam of sunlight, Patti hoped that he would say something that would give definition to what had happened so spontaneously. But he avoided her eyes and dressed quietly. And she, too, didn't know what to say.

***

Tom confronted Alex that night when he came down for supper, "So what are you up to now?"

"The details don't matter, but you should be pleased with the results."

"What results?"

"Check your email."

"My email?"

"You should have a message from OSDA."

"OSDA?"

"Off-Shore Software Development Associates, in Mumbai," Alex explained patiently. "That's the outfit that got the outsourcing contract that lost you your job."

"But who—"

"Just read your email."

"Okay, already."

"Is it there?"

"Yes."

"And it says?"

"They want to interview me for a job. Tomorrow. An online meeting with the head recruiter in Mumbai and the software engineering manager, wherever he is. With video and audio, only..."

"You can borrow my web cam and my headset, too, if you like."

"But how—"

"Good stuff happens."

Marge interjected, "The bumper stickers I read say something different."

"Maybe you've been reading the wrong bumper stickers," Alex suggested. "Lighten up."

"Okay," said Marge. "I'll hit the gym again, while you guys decide the fate of the world."

Tom focused on Alex. "So what should I say tomorrow? How should I spin it to get this job?"

***

That night Patti asked Alex, "So with a few clicks of your magic mouse, you get Tom a job with a company in India?"

"Not a job yet, just a chance for one," Alex corrected her. "It depends on him. OSDA isn't doling out charity. They have work that needs to be done, and Tom has done that same kind of work before and done it well. As outsourcers, they could cut through the bureaucratic bullshit that Tom had to work with in the past. His review cycle would be shorter, and he wouldn't have to waste time in face-to-face meetings. If he works at the same pace he did before, he could be 50% more productive. So they could pay him 25% more than he was making before, and they'd come out ahead."

"And you know this much about Tom and that company because ...?"

"Because of friends and friends of friends. And because I had ages up there in the attic on this beautiful WiFi hot spot to put the pieces together."

"And from this you get ...?"

"Nothing tangible. That's normal. If Tom gets the job, he's happy. If he does solid work, like he always did in the past, OSDA is happy. Happiness makes the world go round."

"Good stuff happens," Patti concluded.

"Exactly."

***

Tom landed the job the next day—in a six-hour PC-based videoconference in which he met and sold himself to two dozen people at half a dozen different locations. His face, which before had been world-weary, now beamed with pride and joy. He started whistling themes from Beethoven, while washing dishes and straightening the kitchen.

To celebrate getting the job, Tom offered to take them all out to another North End Italian restaurant. But, at the last minute, Alex and Patti said they were tied up, so Tom went with just Marge.

When she emerged from her room in a full-length black dress, Tom quickly ducked back to his room and put on a sports jacket and tie, wearing those for the first time in years. Patti snapped pictures of them before they left as if they were going to a high school prom.

***

After Tom started the job, he continued with the same routine, walking Marge to work, and then spending the day at the gym, where she would join him later. He brought along his laptop and worked from there. He had promised himself that he wouldn't bring work home, which, he figured, had led to the breakdown of his marriage.

At breakfast and dinner, he proudly talked about his work and his long-distance co-workers, and the engineering challenges he faced.

18 ~ The Cape of Good Hope

On a Friday morning about a month after Tracy left, Tom got an email from Diane saying, "Call me. Please. Now."

He did.

"Long time no hear from," she said.

"Time flies, but not all files are easy to swat."

"Since when did you become a wit?"

"People change. Like you sending email. That's not your style."

"I didn't have a choice. You disconnected our phone."

"My phone?"

"Whatever phone—the number we shared for nearly twenty-five years."

"Twenty-three to be exact."

"You disconnected the phone and didn't tell me."

"I changed the number. And I did tell you. I left a message on your machine."

"You must have left it on someone else's machine."

"Someone else named Diane who had your voice?"

"Drop it. Drop everything. And get on down here."

"Why?"

"You don't need a why. It's urgent. I need to talk to you face-to-face. Just rent a car and drive on down here. You could be here by lunch."

"But ..."

She hung up.

He left immediately. He was on Route 3 headed south before it occurred to him that he should have called Marge at work to let her know where he was going. But he told himself, he'd be back so early that she wouldn't know that he'd ever gone. He could tell her tonight when he knew what this was about.

He speculated—were the kids in an accident? Was Diane seriously ill? He didn't know yet, and Marge—not knowing Diane—wouldn't understand why he didn't know. He didn't want to upset Marge unnecessarily. They were getting along so well. And she might misunderstand his relationship with his ex. She might think Diane was making a play for him to come back to her, and that he'd consider that possibility. A few months ago, before Tracy, before Marge, he'd have raced to Diane if she had given him the slightest hope. He'd have rented a car and driven down to the Cape as fast as possible, just like he was doing now. Only now he was doing it because of some unnamed emergency.

Diane was out of his life now, except for their common concern for their kids. He no longer had nightmares about her showing up at the apartment. He no longer fantasized about her when intoxicated. His new job was going fine. Money was no longer an issue.

Sure, he had fallen apart when Diane left and he lost his job. He had been in a haze for months, living on take-out and beer, playing endless games of Free Cell and Sudoku, even watching soap operas. He hadn't had the ambition or the self-respect to plan ahead or to do anything to improve his situation—even to buy a bed.

But now, after Tracy left and he got the job, with Marge and Alex and Patti, he felt like a family man again, with a daily routine, and responsibilities, and intelligent people to talk to.

He and Marge were friendly, with occasional flirtatious flares. He believed they could, over time, grow closer. He thought that she wanted that to happen, too. Living in the same apartment, there was no need to rush things—it wasn't like they had to make a date to enjoy one another's company. That was part of the charm of the situation—the comfort level, without any need to "define the relationship." He hated the way that word "relationship" was used these days. If you enjoyed one moment after the other, that could add up to having a good life, without ever having to define anything.

He had particularly enjoyed last night, sitting on the sofa in the kitchen, watching rented DVDs of *Sleepless in Seattle* and *You've Got Mail* on the big-screen TV. Meg Ryan always put him in a romantic mood, and there was something about Marge, despite her height, that reminded him of Meg. By the end of the movies, her head was resting on his shoulder, as if they were a happily married couple, content with the everyday routine of their lives together.

That was when Marge suggested that they go to the attic.

He took her words literally and mentioned that Alex was up there, and maybe Patti, too. She looked back at him, exasperated. He wasn't sure why until after he had heated up left-over pizza for the two of them and gone to bed. Then he remembered something she had told him about her life as a teenager in Arizona—she and her old boyfriend had used "going to the attic" as a euphemism for having sex. Could she have meant that?

And Alex and Patti, what were they doing up in the attic? No way. The two of them were good friends. He was delighted at how well this living arrangement was working out. Alex had convinced Patti to take more challenging courses and went out of his way to walk her back and forth to BU for her safety. And she said she gave him pep talks on those walks, helping him become more sociable, less reclusive. Tom suspected that Patti would soon be setting Alex up for dates with friends of hers from BU.

It seemed strange, though, that Patti herself wasn't dating yet. Maybe being so bright and aggressive scared guys off. No, she probably hadn't found the right guy yet. And being seen with Alex probably scared away guys she didn't want to be hassled by. She was in no hurry.

Marge wasn't in a hurry either. At least that's what he thought until that remark last night, which he may have misinterpreted. Maybe it was time to get closer. Maybe tonight—presuming that Diane's "emergency" wasn't a real emergency. Diane was probably reaching out to him just to slap him in the face and remind him that she still hated his guts. How could he have lived with her for twenty-three years?

Maybe Marge's theory explained it. Last night she said that mature love, like in *Sleepless in Seattle*, was different from young love. She thought teenage love is mostly a matter of curiosity and hormones.

"Hey, don't knock young love," he had objected. "I've got some great memories and I built a life on that foundation—twenty-three years of marriage and two kids. That wasn't just an illusion."

"I'm not saying that's not real, just that it's different. Young love starts from a random pairing and grows over time. Mature love is found."

She explained that when two young people are attracted to one another, they are like emotional stem cells. Regardless of how different they might be to begin with, they can grow together and become a lasting couple.

Mature love between two experienced adults is a different ballgame. When mature adults are attracted to one another, they play it safe—not wanting to do or say anything that would wreck the opportunity. They get to know one another like a soldier might learn how to walk through a mine field—staying away from everything that could trigger the wrong memories and wreck a romantic mood. Their approach to one another is practical, and success is measured in terms of mutual sensual gratification.

But sometimes, two mature people are willing to take the risk of opening up to one another. Then if they're lucky, and don't hit land mines, they can learn the dark corridors of one another's memories, and eventually achieve a magical compatibility.

"Corridors? You mean like in an attic?" Tom had asked, once again forgetting Marge's attic association. Maybe that was one of her *land mines*.

"I mean something bigger than an attic—sprawling, like the terminals at an airport, with tunnels and corridors connecting one building to another."

He was so involved in this memory that he almost missed the exit for Chatham.

Diane was waiting for him on the front lawn, in short shorts and halter top. Her hair, which she had dyed Maureen-O'Hara red, one of her favorite colors, shone against the deep dark tan of her shoulders. Over the years, she had gotten tense and irritable, with eyes held half-shut, and her taut facial muscles making deep crows-feet and forehead wrinkles. Now her face looked relaxed. Her bright green eyes wide-open, the wrinkles hardly noticeable. She hadn't looked that good in decades, and clearly she knew how good she looked.

"How are you doing?" he asked awkwardly, walking toward her. He was disoriented. She was shorter than he remembered. His eyes automatically aimed at where Marge's eyes would be, and focused at her hairline, until he forced himself to look lower. He didn't know what to do with his hands—to hug her or to offer to shake her hand.

She took hold of his shoulders and kissed him quickly on both cheeks.

"I've lost thirty pounds, read a hundred books, stopped smoking, stopped drinking, and found inner peace. What about you?" she asked.

"Well, I've got a new job with a company in India, I've started a harem, and I'm close to finding the meaning of life, the universe, and everything."

"Only close?" she joked back. "I thought you could do better than that. And what's the answer you're working on?"

"I left it on your answering machine."

"Sure. Probably the same time you left me your new phone number."

"Can I help it if you erase your messages unheard?"

"I didn't erase any such message. The message was never on the machine."

"Well, someone must have erased it. Who has been here?"

"So now you're jealous?"

"Well, someone could have broken in."

"To mess with my answering machine? Hell! You're paranoid."

"Crazier things have happened."

"And the answer is yes—not to the answering machine, but to the break-in. That's why I called. No valuables are missing—nothing to report to the police or the insurance company. Whoever it was just took personal items—papers, journals, pictures. He stole memories I wasn't ready to give up. At first I wasn't going to do anything about it. Then I got talking to Ease."

"Ease? What kind of name is that?"

"I think it's initials—E and Z. But everybody calls him Ease. I met him jogging on the beach months ago. He's recovering from the breakup of his marriage. Everybody's divorced these days. And, no, he wasn't coming on to me, though I thought so at first. He's still faithful to his wife, his ex-wife. He thinks a marriage should be eternal regardless of divorces, even regardless of death. It's a religious thing. Anyway, he's become a good friend. He helped me realize that the way I felt about losing those memories was a symptom, that part of me was still holding on to the past, that I didn't want it all to be over."

"And that's a bad thing?" Tom asked, slow to catch the direction of her thoughts. He was out of practice talking to Diane.

"No. A good thing," she insisted.

That was when he noticed that she was wearing her old engagement and wedding rings.

She took his hand and led him down to the beach. There they kicked off their shoes and walked in ankle-deep water along the shore, enjoying the Indian-summer sun.

He had expected her to grill him about Marge and Patti and his new job. Inevitably, she would find new ways to belittle him.

Instead, she said nothing, and led him a few hundred yards from Forest Beach Road to a breakwater from which they could see for miles in all directions. There they sat on the rocks for hours and watched the waves come in and the boats go by. It was like his first night with Tracy, only without words.

He couldn't remember ever feeling this relaxed with Diane before.

19 ~ The Return of Diane

On the way back from the Cape, Tom considered calling Marge at work to let her know where he had been. But he had left his cell phone at home and didn't want to stop and hunt for a pay phone. These days, pay phones were scarce in the city, much less along the highway. Besides, it was still early. He could get to Gold's Gym before she did, in which case, there would be no need for explanation.

But an accident ahead on Route 3 held him up. and by the time he got to the Southeast Expressway, it was rush hour.

He spent his time in traffic composing one speech after another—all of which made him sound guilty, when he hadn't done anything wrong.

He hadn't so much as kissed Diane, had hardly talked to her. He had just sat with her by the sea. Why did he feel so guilty about it?

It wasn't as if he was married to Marge; but it felt good living with her, the way they were, and he didn't want to disturb the delicate balance. They were still in "mine-field" mode, as Marge would say. He hoped that their feelings for one another could grow gradually, without any immediate need for commitment.

But the hint that he might consider getting back together with Diane could wreck whatever might have been possible with Marge. Better that he not say anything about this trip. Getting home an hour or more after Marge, he'd have to come up with some plausible excuse—a face-to-face business meeting in the suburbs, on the South Shore. He hadn't mentioned it because it would be short, and he'd be home early. He got hung up in traffic. Yes, talk about the traffic. With any luck, there would be a mention of this traffic mess on the evening news.

As it turned out, when Tom arrived, Marge and Alex were washing the dinner dishes, and talking about the upcoming Patriots game. Marge microwaved the spaghetti they had saved for him and went back to her conversation with Alex. To his relief, she didn't ask for an explanation; so he didn't provide one.

As he regained his equanimity, stuffing himself with second helpings, and enjoying a freezer-chilled beer, he noticed that there was something different about Marge. The hair—yes, he was proud to have noticed the hair this time . She had dyed it the same shade that Diane had dyed hers, that shade of red that looked like Maureen O'Hara—she must have used one of the bottles of hair color that Diane had left behind. He nearly spilled his beer. It was too much of a coincidence—seeing the two of them with that same shade of hair on the same day, and realizing that while it looked great on Diane, who in the right light resembled Maureen O'Hara in *Parent Trap*; it looked artificial, and wig-like on Marge.

If he complimented her, he'd come across as insincere—he hated this look. But if he didn't say anything that would mean that he wasn't paying attention to her looks.

As it was, she didn't say a thing. And since it was a Friday night and she didn't have to go to the office in the morning, they stayed up most of the night watching more Meg Ryan videos—*Prelude to a Kiss*, *Kate and Leopold*, and *French Kiss*.

It felt good sitting beside her on the sofa, with her head resting on his shoulder—at least as good as sitting on the rocks by the sea with Diane.

***

Saturday at noon, all four of them were in the kitchen sipping their first cup of coffee and checking the news on their laptops, when they heard a key turn in the door. Alex dashed to grab the ladder to the attic. Patti and Marge turned toward the door, tense. Tom shouted, "Who's there?"

But before he had finished saying the words, Diane strode into the room, like she lived there.

"Diane?" Tom muttered in disbelief.

"So this is the famous Diane?" noted Marge sizing her up and doing a double-take at the color of her hair, before stepping forward to shake her hand, bending down to Diane's height, emphasizing the difference.

Tom tried to signal Diane to hush, wanting to have a minute alone with her to ask her not to say anything about his visit yesterday.

Diane winked in his direction, as if she understood, then, taking note of Marge's hair color, responded, "And you must be Marge. Tom has told me so much about you."

"He has? I didn't know..."

"Yes, of course, why even yesterday down at the Cape."

"But Tom wasn't—"

"It was such a beautiful Indian-summer day. Great for wading and sitting on the rocks and enjoying the peaceful rhythm of the waves. Of course he told you about our day?"

"Of course," Marge answered, improvising.

"You have a key?" Alex called, from half-way up the ladder to the attic.

"Alex? Yes, you must be Alex. Tom has told me so much about you, as well." They walked toward each other and shook hands, while Tom tried to sort out what was going on—he had never mentioned Alex to Diane and had no idea how she could have heard about him.

"The key?" Alex repeated, with evident concern.

"Yes, of course, I have a key."

"And who else has keys?" Alex asked Tom.

"The kids," Tom offered.

"And the tenants downstairs have keys to the front door?"

"Of course," Diane answered.

"And the lock on the front door hasn't been changed in recent memory?"

"Not as long as I can remember," Tom admitted.

"Then dozens of people have had opportunities to make copies."

"So this is where the paranoia epidemic began," Diane noted. "Tom was so paranoid yesterday about phone numbers and answering machines. There's no need to be afraid, Tom dear," she reassured him, grasping his chin like she might have done with a child who was upset for no good reason. "The world is not a scary place."

"So what brings you to town?" asked Marge, in a tone that Tom thought was polite and considerate, given the circumstances.

"Memories. Seeing Tom yesterday brought back so many memories, I woke up knowing that I had to have some of the things that I had left behind in the attic— relics of our time. I thought you'd probably be sleeping in." She glanced from Marge to Tom and back. He tried not to look guilty, though he had no reason to feel guilty. "So rather than call and disturb you, I jumped in the car and drove up.

"Oh, I see you've been decorating," Diane noted. But she wasn't looking at the new kitchen table and chairs or the fact that the TV and sofa were in the kitchen or that the former living room was partitioned off with sliding doors. Rather she was staring at the Hopi-style dream catchers hanging by doorways.

"Those?" asked Marge. "Yes, that's my contribution to the house. Relics of my heritage—from Arizona, near reservations."

"Charming, I'm sure," Diane acknowledged, then turned to Tom. "Tom, dear, could you come up with me to the attic. You've probably moved things around up there, and I'll need your help finding what I want."

Tom hesitated. Did Marge cringe at that phrase? The notion of "going to the attic" with Diane felt strange, given what he had been thinking about Marge. And he had a momentary flashback to college days when he and Diane had slipped up there for privacy.

Diane started up, not waiting for a reply, presuming that Tom would follow. Half-way up, she asked, loudly, "Have you shown Marge the attic?"

"Yes, of course," Tom answered quickly, before recognizing his words could be taken in another sense.

"The view is lovely up there," Marge added.

"Yes, indeed," Diane countered. "I'm glad you're taking full advantage of the opportunity while you're here."

Tom, not wanting to look Marge in the eye, followed Diane.

"What are these?" Diane asked pointedly from the top of the ladder.

"You probably mean the Kachina," Marge shouted from the kitchen. "My contribution as well. Those are magic Hopi dolls, to make those who live here prosperous and happy."

"Of course," Diane countered. "How quaint. Kachina. I'll have to check that on the Web. I volunteer at a nursery school in Chatham. I'm sure the kids would love to make little things like that."

Once he reached the top, Tom ventured to ask, "What exactly are you looking for?"

"Oh, that can wait, Tom. It's been so long since I was up here last. And the cupola, I don't think I've been up there for years. It's such a beautiful day, and the view is great, as Marge just reminded me. Come on," she coaxed him, as she started climbing to the cupola.

She took his hand, so he would help her up, and kept holding it when they reached the top, and stood there, quietly. He felt at peace with her as he had yesterday at the beach. All the embarrassment and confusion of Diane's unexpected arrival faded away. They didn't need to talk.

An ambulance racing up the street broke the spell, and Tom realized that more than an hour had passed. He started down the ladder, asking, without daring to look back and meet her eyes, "What was it you were looking for?"

"That's all right," she answered, hurrying after him. "We'll get to that soon enough. I'm in no hurry."

Back down in the attic, she closed the trap door before Tom got to it. She took his hand again, led him to the old piano, and started playing and singing "I am I, Don Quixote, the Man of La Mancha ..."

He sang along, one show song after another. Another ambulance passed, and he stopped abruptly, brought back to here and now. They had been up here a long time. Marge must have heard the music. He opened the trap door and scrambled down the ladder. "I have to check my email," he muttered a lame excuse. "I'm expecting an important message."

Marge was in the kitchen, whistling those same *Man of La Mancha* tunes. Tom was amazed at how calm she seemed. But she was scrubbing the kitchen sink and counters hard and repeatedly. Maybe she was embarrassed that the place wasn't looking spiffy for the "ex."

Her eyes met his. He hated having put her through this. He knew then that he didn't want to go back to his old life.

She dropped her scouring pad, wiped her hands, and pushed her hair back out of her eyes, then laughed remembering the color.

"It's terrible isn't it?" she asked. "Patti suggested I try green next time."

"On you, green, blue, pink—any color would be beautiful."

They walked toward each other and hugged.

"Do you want to go to the attic?" Tom asked, looking her straight in the eye.

"Your room or mine?" she answered.

They didn't kiss until they were on his mattress.

And they went about their business as if they had both been wanting to do this for a long time, and as if the rest of the world simply didn't matter.

Diane slammed the front door as she left. But neither Tom nor Marge took any note of that.

When Tom came the first time, he muttered, "I love you. Will you marry me?"

Maybe Marge didn't hear him. She didn't acknowledge his words. He hoped she didn't hear. He hadn't planned to say that. He didn't know if he meant it. He hadn't had time to sort out thoughts like that. It was too soon. He didn't want to scare her away. And he didn't think he was ready for commitment. It was another one of those land mines mature lovers stumble onto. With Diane, when they were first married, before the kids, he had gotten into the habit of saying that automatically when he came with her. And it had just happened now, like somebody had pushed a button and started playing an old tape.

But she didn't answer. Thank God she didn't answer. That meant that if she had heard she could pretend she hadn't, and he could pretend it hadn't happened at all.

20 ~ Jack Attack

After Tom's inadvertent "proposal", Marge dreamt she was trapped in a deep dungeon. The only way out was to stack furniture so she could climb up to the window. But there was no furniture, not even a bed, just a mattress on the floor.

She had deliberately ignored Tom's words. She didn't know if he meant them, or if it was an automatic response she had triggered. And she wasn't ready to define her relationship with him and make plans. She was relieved that he didn't insist on an answer from her. It was best forgotten. Let everything proceed slowly, and that might some day be the right question. Rushing to commitment could wreck everything.

Then again, she wondered about the dream; and she wondered about Jack. She had the nagging feeling that it might have been her, not Jack, who had the problem about commitment. Or maybe both of them—maybe they had that in common.

No, she was theorizing too much. She needed to be more spontaneous. And she had to do something about this hair—it was a horrid shade, and, to make matters worse, the same shade as Diane's. "Green" she had said to Tom. Yes, she remembered Patti had some trick hair color—wild colors that were easy to wash out.

She slipped out of bed and went to talk to Patti.

An hour later, when Tom and, shortly afterward, Alex staggered wearily out of their rooms, Marge and Patti were sitting peacefully at the kitchen table reading the Sunday Globe and sipping coffee, both with bright green hair.

Neither Tom nor Alex said anything about the hair—Tom on purpose and Alex because he didn't notice.

Tom got himself a bowl of Cheerios, and Alex made toast and poached half a dozen eggs for himself.

So Marge said to Patti, "Don't you just love it?"

"Absolutely. I can't wait to see the reactions in class tomorrow."

"I have a dress that's the same shade."

"I think I'll wear a black sweater and black jeans. Black goes with any color."

Tom kept staring at the sports section of the paper, playing it safe, holding the paper high to shield his reaction. Marge suspected that if she kept this color, he would never say a word about it—he was still in landmine mode, not knowing her well enough to be sure this was a joke.

When Alex finally noticed, he dropped his plate of eggs on the floor.

Patti hugged him, gave him a quick kiss, and helped him clean up the mess.

Tom and Marge had never seen them react that way to one another—did they have something going? All that time in the attic together?

"Okay, Tom," Marge said. "'Ollie, Ollie, oxen free.' You can stop hiding now. The game's over."

He put his paper down, with an embarrassed look and said in mock seriousness, "Your hair is lovely this morning."

"Almost as lovely as yesterday, don't you think?"

Finally, he dared to laugh.

Half an hour later their hair was back to normal.

That's when the doorbell rang.

It was Jack, Marge's old boyfriend.

Jack was built like a professional basketball player. He towered over Tom, who had always considered himself tall, but had never come face-to-face with someone this size.

"How did you find me here?" Marge challenged him.

"Your cell phone was disconnected."

"I changed the number."

"So I got your address from a mutual friend."

"What mutual friend? I haven't been telling people."

"Hey, I don't want to make trouble. Just a friend."

"And what brings you here?"

"I'd like to talk."

"So talk."

"In private."

"You can talk here. These are my friends. We keep no secrets."

"Anywhere but the kitchen, please."

"So now you're allergic to kitchens? You've changed a lot in a short time."

"Please."

She led him to her room.

"Is he the one?"

"Who?"

"Tom."

"The what?"

"The guy you were seeing before, when you were living with me?"

"How many times do I have to tell you—there was no other man."

"Past tense?"

"None of your business. Tom is my landlord and my good friend. We met the day I showed up at the door looking for a room to rent— a few months ago."

"Sure. Whatever you say. I didn't come here to argue with you."

"Then what?"

"I finally realized that it doesn't matter."

"What doesn't matter?"

"Whatever you did or didn't do, I still love you. I want you back."

"You've got to be kidding."

"Even the commitment thing, the ring and all that. That's all on the table."

"Isn't this a bit sudden? I mean, ten years of dancing away from that, and now, months after we broke up, you suddenly are ready for commitment?"

"I can see you've changed. And I can't sit back and wait. I want you, and it has to be now before you change so much I wouldn't know you anymore."

"You must be nuts. Out of the blue, on a Sunday morning, you come barging in and as much as propose to me?"

"Think about it. You don't need to answer me now. But I can see that you and Tom are getting close, and I want to put my bid in before the bidding's closed."

"Such a romantic image. You always were poetic."

"And while you're thinking about it, remember that you know me far better than you know Tom, and he may not be quite what you think he is."

"Meaning?"

"The whole time we lived together, I was faithful to you."

"Meaning?"

"Tom's not so much a straight arrow as you may think."

"And what the hell would you know about Tom?"

"Ask him about Meeghan."

"Meeghan? What Meeghan? His ex-wife is named Diane. There was Tracy, but she's gone."

"Yes, yes. I know."

"How would you know? What mutual friend would know that?"

"Just ask him about Meeghan from Flanagan's. And then think again about my offer. That's all—take a good look at his past, and then decide what you think about me."

He left without waiting for her to reply. Going out the front door he called back, "Forget the green. It looked terrible, and it wasn't funny. That just isn't you."

He was gone before it dawned on Marge that he had no way of knowing that she had dyed her hair green that morning. She ran to a mirror—there were no traces of the dye left. He couldn't possibly know.

"What was that about?" asked Tom.

"Just my ex being my ex. Like yesterday with your ex."

"I guess this must be an ex-rated weekend," Tom ventured.

"Get over here," she insisted, pulling him into her room.

He followed her quickly, guessing that this encounter might have turned her on.

"Who is Meeghan?" she asked once she had shut her door.

"Meeghan? What Meeghan?"

"Meeghan from Flanagan's."

"Oh, that Meeghan. She doesn't matter."

"You slept with her?"

"Yes," Tom admitted reluctantly.

"More than once?"

"Yes."

"Over the course of months?"

"Yes."

"So there might have been some connection between Meeghan and your breakup with Diane?"

"It was a symptom, not a cause. Our marriage was already over by then."

"But Diane's leaving came as a total shock—that's what you said before."

"Look, Meeghan doesn't matter. You don't see her around now do you?"

"That might be more her choice than yours. And what else haven't you told me?"

"Easy does it."

"Don't say that. Don't ever say that!"

"And how did you hear about Meeghan? Something like that doesn't show up in a Google search. Did you hire a private eye or something?"

"Jack told me."

"Jack? And how would Jack know? No one but Diane and Meeghan herself knew about that, and they have no connection with him."

"Don't try to sidetrack me. We're talking about you and Meeghan, not about Jack."

"Okay already. Meeghan was this waitress at Flanagan's, before Tracy came to town. She remembered my name, and always had something friendly to say when I saw her there; and she'd remember what I'd told her the last time and ask follow-up questions. She was fun to talk to."

"And probably fun to look at."

"That too," he admitted. "She was a single mother in her late twenties. She had a day job as a secretary for an insurance company. A cute kid."

"Her or her child?"

"Both."

"So you saw her at her apartment?"

"She was studying computer programming, weekends at Suffolk. She asked me questions from her classes. And it got to be a regular thing that we'd sit together at Flanagan's to talk about that. But that wasn't enough time. After all, she was supposed to be working when she was there. So she asked me to stop by her apartment."

"So she was coming on to you, not vice versa?"

"Okay, I didn't object. I wanted to help. I enjoyed helping."

"I'm sure you did. And do you still *help* her?"

"That all ended last year. She finished her computer course and switched to art history."

"And where is she now?"

"She left town. Tracy got her old job. That's the same Meeghan who told Tracy about San Francisco."

"And she was the only one, right?"

"Yes, yes."

"And all this phone business—that's just a random idiot harassing us? That has nothing to do with you and some secret in your past? That's not some other ex or a love child looking for her daddy?"

"Nothing like that."

"I want to believe you."

"What you see is what you get."

"I'm just concerned about what I don't see."

That night they went to bed together in her room, and she felt compelled to tell him about her past, in hopes that that would make him more willing to share his with her. She told him what she had told Tracy—the tale of her childhood in Arizona, her controlling father, and Zeke, the boyfriend who tried to trap her into eternal marriage.

Tom listened attentively, caressing and kissing her as she talked. He showed no sign of jealousy; rather, the tale of her early sexual experiences seemed to turn him on.

As they got warmer and closer, Jack and what Jack had said faded in her mind, and she no longer felt the need to get Tom to open up about his past. He guessed that the time was right and got up to get condoms from his room.

Alone for a couple minutes, she grew irritated. She remembered he had had condoms within reach the first time they did it, in his room. For all she knew, he might always keep a supply on hand in case he got "lucky" with whatever woman he happened to be with.

She really didn't know this man. She had gotten involved too fast. She would turn him down when he came back in her room. They shouldn't do it now. She needed time to think.

But before she had a chance to tell him that, Patti and Alex returned—after the date with Ollie and the attack in the Common.

While Alex told Tom and Marge what had happened, including the business about the earphones that looked like earrings, Patti paced around the kitchen, inspecting the ceiling, then she grabbed the pole they used to open the trap door. With it, she knocked down a little black gadget from the corner.

"God," Alex exclaimed. "It's a web cam."

Patti slapped him and scratched him. "Why did you do it? Why? And what else did you do? Are there web cams everywhere? Did you put one in the shower? Is there one in the toilet bowl? How perverse are you, bastard?"

Before Tom and Marge could pull her back or Alex could squirm away, the phone rang, and Patti rushed to answer it. She pushed the speaker phone button and screamed, "You fiend. And you actually dare call here after that?"

But it wasn't the assailant, it was Tom's ex-wife Diane.

"Patti, are you all right? You didn't look like you were badly hurt."

"Look? What do you mean look? You can't see me."

"But of course I could. At least there's some good that came from that Internet nonsense you're involved in. But now the image is coming from a strange angle. I can't see you anymore."

"What web site are you looking at?"

"Why yours, of course. I don't understand why you do it—I mean in nearly twenty-five years of marriage I never imagined that Tom was an exhibitionist, but this reality TV and web cam stuff is beyond me. I guess it must be some kind of ego trip."

"What web site?"

"Haremscarem.com of course."

Alex picked up the web cam and Tom brought his laptop over to the phone so Patti could see. As Alex pointed the cam at each of them in succession, their images appeared on the screen.

"How did you find that site?" Patti asked. She heard her voice echoed from the laptop a second later.

Diane answered, "A neighbor chanced on it and told me."

There was no off switch on the web cam, and it was wirelessly connected, so Alex put it in a trash bag and the screen went black. Then Tom smashed it with a hammer, and the audio went dead.

Alex was as shocked as the rest of them. He hadn't done it. And if it hadn't been for him and his cell phone trick, Patti might be in the morgue right now.

They brainstormed the rest of the afternoon and speculated that the gas man had set up the web cam and connected it wirelessly to Tom's desktop computer which was on all the time. From there, by WiFi, the images and sound went to the Web page where Diane had seen them.

But who was the gas man? And why would he have picked this apartment as a target?

Tom mentioned the stranger he had met at Flanagan's, soon after they had all moved in.

Marge noted, "You seem to get into a lot of trouble at Flanagan's. Maybe it's time you stopped going there."

But how would Diane and Jack have found the site? Alex suggested search engines and blogs. The assailant from the Boston Common might have found it that way, by chance. But Diane and Jack wouldn't have.

Maybe the gas man was casing the apartment, planning a burglary. But a would-be burglar wouldn't put a public web cam in an apartment he intended to hit.

From their height and build, the gas man, the stranger at Flanagan's, and the assailant were three different people. Disguise couldn't account for the differences. But what was the connection among them? Grudges against Alex or Marge or Patti or Tom? Or were they hired by someone with a grudge?

21 ~ Easy Does It

Patti stayed home from school for a week. Too much was going on. Too much was still unknown.

Marge was spooked, too.

As usual, Tom walked her to work. Now he met her there after work and walked her to the gym. But she still went out to lunch alone, at odd times, depending on her schedule and workload.

Two days in a row she sensed that she was being followed on her way to her favorite pizza shop on Newbury Street. The first time she didn't say anything about it to the others—it must be just her imagination. This wasn't a lone guy in a coat with the collar high to disguise his face. Rather, it was a clean-cut young guy in jeans, with bulky sweaters under a jean jacket; and a petite brunette, in a longish skirt and a white blouse, and a heavy winter coat on top. They were dressed too heavily for the mild weather. They looked like newly arrived tourists, used to a warmer climate, to whom an Indian summer in Boston felt like winter.

When she spotted them again the next day, she panicked, ducked into a dress shop, and tried calling Tom. But the battery on her cell phone had run down, and the store didn't have a public phone. The nearest public phone was outside the Library in Copley Square, four blocks away. When she came out of the shop, they were waiting for her. She sprinted up the street, and they sprinted after her. She turned and they turned. In the crunch of lunchtime pedestrians, she lost them on Boylston Street. She decided to head back to work without lunch.

Then as she crossed with the walk light at the corner of Boylston and Dartmouth Streets, they were standing right in her path, waiting for her. Pushed along by the crowd of pedestrians, she passed within a few feet of them, then lost them again, racing zig-zag through the crowd.

For the rest of the week she took a bag lunch. She couldn't tolerate any more of this.

Tom had checked the apartment thoroughly by sight, and Alex had double-checked with a gadget that detects wireless signals. There were no more web cams.

Alex checked the domain-name registry to see who owned haremscarem.com, but it was in the name of an Internet service provider that protected the anonymity of its customers. All they'd tell him was that the account had been closed.

Diane no longer called and no longer stopped by unannounced.

Jack, too, backed off from Marge.

Ollie, probably embarrassed at his cowardice, stayed away from Patti.

It had been weeks since Alex had heard anything from his old drop-ship partners.

Marge sometimes spotted that odd couple in the distance, but they didn't come close with Tom around.

The four of them settled into a new routine, with Alex shadowing Patti and Tom shadowing Marge, and everything seemed okay. This should have been a time to recover and get on with their lives. But Marge still felt tense. Whenever she entered a room—even at the office—she checked the ceiling for web cams. And she woke up repeatedly at night, dreaming about her father and Zeke in Arizona.

She had always blamed Zeke for colluding with her father so they would be "caught in the act" and she would be forced to marry young and stay in the Mormon faith and in Arizona. But maybe it wasn't a trap of Zeke's. Maybe Dad chanced upon them, and Zeke was just making the best of the situation. Maybe it was Dad—with that killer instinct of his; Dad acting as God's representative on Earth who was trying to trap the two of them.

She needed to talk about those times, to sort out who she was and who she wanted to be. Tom sat on the sofa with her, as he had before when she wanted to share memories. He listened, but was cautious in his responses, sensing her tension. He was interested in what she said but he didn't want to accidentally set off a land mine by his reactions. His puzzled looks alienated her, but she needed to talk this out.

"I'm no longer a Mormon. I theorized myself out of it back in college, but it's still in my blood. I feel an emotional bond with a huge extended family back there. You have no idea ..."

"Please try to help me understand."

"Imagine a family reunion, outdoors, on a farm."

"Well, I haven't been on a farm, but I remember family reunions at the Cape. Barbeques. Pick-up football games with cousins."

"Okay. That's the general idea. But instead of dozens of cousins, imagine three hundred of them."

"Oh."

"A very big family. A very different experience. Everyone for miles around was a relative of some flavor or another. Everybody knew me. Everybody watched out for me. Dad always said, 'God is watching you.' And that was easy to believe because family was watching me, everywhere, and God was another flavor of family.

"Last night I dreamt that web cams with angel wings were hovering overhead. Then I saw God, the way I used to imagine him—like Dad, only his beard was longer and completely white. He was sitting on a cloud-like throne with a laptop computer. And on the screen he was watching me and you, naked in bed."

"That's scary."

"And at the same time, it's comforting."

"What do you mean?"

"I miss the childhood sense of being connected to everyone and everything. I even miss the feeling of guilt. I miss the belief that everything I do matters, that my life is a battleground of good and evil. That God knows and cares when I sin, just as Dad did.

"When I woke up from that dream, I felt bad that the web cam was gone. Even when we didn't know that it was in the kitchen, we were wirelessly connected to everyone in the world. Anyone with a web connection could see and hear us whenever they wanted. That was a hateful invasion of privacy. But at the same time it awoke nostalgia for my childhood when I felt connected with relatives, ancestors, fellow believers, and even with God. Even when I forgot them, they were connected with me. God was watching. My life had meaning because of that social context, and my immediate family community stretched back over a hundred years. The same year that Pru went west by stagecoach, my ancestors set out on foot along a similar route, from Iowa City to Salt Lake City, pushing wheelbarrows and carts stuffed with all their worldly goods. Many of those people died during that trek. They were willing to suffer any hardship to reach the promised land. A few months later the transcontinental railroad was completed, and they could have gone that same distance quickly and cheaply. But they and their descendants were proud of their accomplishment in having walked it. Their merit was all the greater for their sacrifice.

"Later, my great-grandfather migrated to northern Arizona with the blessing of the Church, and irrigated the desert, turning wasteland into farmland with the help of his ten wives and fifty children. It was like the Jews returning to Israel after World War II. His oldest son married after polygamy was outlawed and fathered fifteen children with a single wife. His oldest, my father, became an elder of the church. The community for twenty miles around turned to him for advice in times of trouble. He had just one child— me—not for lack of wanting more. Mom had half a dozen miscarriages before she died in a car crash.

"Dad didn't want to lose me. He thought that if I went away to college, I would come under godless influence and never return. And he was right.

"He wanted to make sure I would carry on the line and that my progeny would too—extending his connectedness by blood and religion far into the future. And, for the price of obedience, he offered me that sense of total belonging.

"I escaped from Dad, from Zeke, from all the expectations and responsibilities of the Mormon community. But I paid a price, and I'm only now beginning to feel the magnitude of the loss.

"Instead of that traditional security, I find myself with a make-shift proto-family that could dissolve at any moment. And the only sense of connectedness this modern world offers is a WiFi connection among exhibitionists and voyeurs."

At her office, Marge found it difficult to concentrate on her work. Why should she care about survey questionnaires about depression in the workplace? She lost track of what she was doing, entered data in the wrong fields, miscalculated correlations, and misplaced files. She daydreamed through staff meetings, seeing not the PowerPoint slides on the screen, but rather the depths of the Grand Canyon, pulling her down to where she belonged.

It came as no surprise when she received an email from Zeke, the man she had nearly married. She presumed that he had psychically sensed her distress. At some essential level, they had always been connected.

His tone was friendly, without expectations, or pressure of any kind. She wrote back telling about her life since Arizona. Zeke was a willing audience, who understood her far better than Tom ever would.

He prompted her to tell all and seemed to know a lot about her already, but she didn't concern herself about how he knew what he knew. Maybe he, too, had watched and heard her by web cam—it seemed like everyone else had found that page—why not him?

He seemed to have the listening skills of a psychotherapist and the generosity of a representative of God on Earth. He had spent five years as a missionary in Argentina and was now an elder of the same congregation as her father.

She felt connected to him, and through him to the relatives she hadn't seen in more than a decade, to all their fellow-believers, to all mankind— past, present, and future.

She tried to describe these feelings to Patti. Hearing about the attack on Patti on the Common had awakened Marge's fears of the dangers of living in a big city and had triggered memories of the town where she had grown up and the messages of community, acceptance, and religious love that Zeke was now reinforcing through his frequent emails.

Patti swapped roles with Marge, calming her, and giving her sound advice. Patti recommended caution and reminded Marge that after all these years this guy would be a very different person and that she shouldn't be so quick to trust him.

Tom was no help at all. He didn't understand what had come over Marge. He listened politely as she explained the tenets of faith of the Church of the Latter Day Saints. She told him how the angel Moroni appeared to Joseph Smith in 1823 and helped him find the gold plates and translate the ancient record they contained. Despite wanting to understand and sympathize, he cringed, as he would have if forced to listen to door-to-door missionaries. He and Marge were no longer in tune with one another.

Without discussing why, Tom and Marge slept in separate rooms. They didn't even watch movies or do Sudoku together. Tom treated her like someone convalescing from a nervous breakdown. He hoped she would go back to being her normal self. He didn't want to do anything that could get in the way of their getting close once again. Meanwhile, he felt very uncomfortable in her presence.

She didn't want to hurt him. But she no longer thought of him as a necessary part of her future life. He was her friend, as Alex and Patti were her friends. But they all had their separate lives and would move on.

22 ~ Waiting for a Jet Plane

Marge insisted on going to the airport alone. She was going for an interview, checking a job possibility Alex, at her request, had uncovered for her near her childhood home. She hadn't made up her mind. This wasn't good-bye, she told them all.

But she felt relieved to leave, however briefly. She needed to get away from the tension and confusion she felt in the apartment. If offered the job, she might grab it. She might even ask Tom to ship her stuff out to there, so she would never have to go back to Boston.

A last encounter with her stalkers pushed her even further in that direction. As she sprinted through the freezing rain and wind to the cab that would take her to the airport, the guy and the girl came at her from different sides. As the girl grabbed her coat, Marge slapped her hand away, slammed the door shut, and shrieked at the driver to go. At least he understood that much English. He didn't seem to understand anything else she said, as she stared out the back window, checking to see if she was being followed.

The taxi driver got lost, then stuck in traffic at the Callahan Tunnel, then dropped her off at Terminal E, the international terminal, instead of Terminal B.

Carry-on suitcase in one hand, briefcase in the other, she raced to get to the check-in counter in time to catch her flight to Phoenix.

Her watch had stopped. Everything had stopped in the nor'easter—the first major storm of the winter, a week before Thanksgiving. That's one aspect of Boston she wouldn't miss.

She found herself in the vast expanse of Logan Airport's Public Parking. What time was it? What floor was she on? Which way to Terminal B Departures?

Somehow she found her way to the American Airline ticket counter thirty minutes before her flight was due to take off. No line here, thank God. But she still had to go through security and sprint to the gate—no way.

Out of breath, she could hardly talk and could hardly hear what the attendant said in response. The flight was delayed—at least an hour—due to the weather.

Heaven be praised.

By the time she made it to the gate—what felt like a half-mile sprint—her flight was delayed another hour.

She collapsed at a table near a bar that served food, not far from a monitor showing departures.

The lights flashed on and off—not a good sign.

The wind outside must be 50 or 60 miles an hour.

She should have called ahead and changed her flight to another day—the interview could be postponed. They said she was perfect for the job. They said this face-to-face interview was just a formality. But she had gotten a special deal on the flight, and it was a non-refundable fare, and the weather outlook was ambiguous. The storm might miss them, and if it hit, it might blow away in an hour.

She needed a drink to relax. Everything was happening too fast.

It would all work out fine, she reassured herself. Dad would be surprised—she hadn't given him a clue about her plans. Zeke would be surprised too, even though he had all the details. His tone was skeptical when he last called her on her cell phone. He challenged her, doubting she would go through with this trip.

She planned to rent a car in Phoenix, then drive to the Grand Canyon on her way home. She wanted to see it again, to feel that irrational pull. Yes, the house where she had grown up was home, not Tom's Back-Bay apartment. This didn't have to make sense. This was reality. Her reality.

All flights were delayed. The tables were crowded. A tall man in a business suit asked if he could sit in the other chair at her table.

She and this guy, Matt, were soon chatting over martinis about weather and sports and politics. She had always had a thing about tall men—men much taller than she. She hadn't gone out with anyone as short as Tom before. Tom and she were about the same height. She sensed that Matt was flirting with her, and she flirted back, asking personal questions. Men love to talk about themselves.

After her third drink, she wasn't paying close attention to what he said. But on automatic pilot, she kept eye contact, smiled, and periodically made acknowledging noises. Part of her was remembering Zeke as she had known him long ago and as he appeared in recent photos he had emailed to her. Another part of her was remembering when she first met Jack, who was nearly as tall as Zeke, on a day as windy, rainy, and cold as today. They were waiting for a subway at Copley Square. He was reading a Robert Parker mystery. They made eye contact and started talking about Spenser's taste for food and their own favorite Boston-area restaurants. Minutes later, they were in a cab together on their way to Legal Seafood by the Marriott Hotel—just a few blocks. She was usually cautious and rational, but like on the night when she and Tom first got close, she felt wildly spontaneous with Jack. Rather than go back to her place or his place, they had spent the night in a room at the Marriott.

As Matt handed her another refill of her martini, she imagined him in a hotel room. Then her rational editor blanked that out just before she heard the name "Meeghan".

He was talking about his wife Meeghan and his daughter Trish. He may have been talking about them for quite a while.

Apparently, Meeghan and he had had some rocky times. But they were back together now, and it was better than ever. He was heading home to her in Chicago, after an extended business trip, selling sports equipment to high schools.

He pulled out his wallet to show her dozens of snapshots of Meeghan and Trish.

Triggered by the name "Meeghan", Marge fetched from her wallet a photo of her and Tom and Alex and Patti in front of Tom's building. She was surprised to hear herself introducing them as her husband and kids. She bragged about each of them—Tom as a star software engineer for a multi-national high-tech company headquartered in India, so good that he could do his work anywhere, remotely. Patti as a gifted writer and a freshman at BU taking all upper-class courses. Alex was an Internet business whiz, who through his connections had helped Tom get his job, and now was helping her get a new job, too.

"What kind of job?"

"Social worker. I've been a social psychologist for the last ten years—developing and interpreting surveys about workplace health and depression. It pays a good salary, but I'm burnt out, and too depressed to write about other people's depression. I need a change," she explained.

"And where?"

"Arizona. That's where I'm headed now. For the final job interview."

"Arizona? I understand that your husband can do his work from anywhere, but what about the kids? Won't they have to stay behind? Won't you miss them? Or will they just pick up and go with you and start fresh out there?"

"No. They won't be going. Not Tom, either. Just me."

"Oh."

Marge started weeping, steadily, as she told him about everything that had happened—the harassing phone calls, the web cam, the attack on Patti at the Boston Common, Tom and his women. As she told it, he had been unfaithful to her, his wife of nearly twenty-five years, with a couple of barmaids. By coincidence, one of them was named Meeghan. After all these years, she couldn't trust him. She was leaving him to go back to where she had grown up and start a new life.

She told Matt about Zeke and her father, and how she hated them both and escaped from them, but that was then and this was now.

Matt was a good listener. He let her talk uninterrupted.

At some point, he left. They must have said goodbye to one another; but with all the martinis she had had, her memory was playing tricks on her.

The other tables were deserted. The bar was locked up behind a metal screen. Had she missed her flight?

She panicked and rushed, off-balance, toward the monitors. She had to stand close and calm down, to slow the swaying of the monitors before she realized that all the flights—not just hers—were marked "cancelled".

To her surprise, she was relieved; no, delighted.

As she stood near the monitors, she saw her mother at the far end of the corridor, at the turn from the gates back toward baggage claim. No, it couldn't be her mother, who had died long ago, but it looked like her. The woman was silently signaling to Marge to come quickly, to leave the airport. Then the woman vanished, or Marge woke up, still standing by the monitors.

She had to go home to her real home—the apartment, to the people who meant most to her and to the man she wanted to spend the rest of her life with—Tom.

They must know by now that the flight had been cancelled. They must be wondering where she was. The battery on her cell phone was dead again. Eventually, she found a working pay phone. But she didn't have the coordination necessary to push the right keys. After waking half a dozen angry strangers with wrong numbers, she didn't have the presence of mind to ask an operator to put through the call for her.

She raced down one corridor after another, wanting to get to the baggage claim area in Arrivals, and out to the street where at least one cab must be available—she hoped—even at this time of night. But she had trouble interpreting the signs and found herself in an enclosed passageway over an empty highway.

She stopped and stared down at the road—thank God for windows, strong windows, protecting her from the wind and the freezing rain and stopping her from falling.

Then a stranger approached her. Where did he come from? Had he followed her? Like her, he was bundled in an overcoat—a traveler, not an employee.

She couldn't run from him in her current state and had no reason to run from him. He hadn't said or done anything threatening. He, too, was probably stuck here by a cancelled flight. He, too, probably wanted a cab. But, instinctively, she knew she shouldn't talk to strangers ... except at a bar, of course, when the stranger was tall, and friendly and handsome. This stranger was tall. But she wasn't in a bar. This was a deserted corridor of a deserted airport, well after midnight. She avoided eye contact, and leaned up against the window, looking out, wondering what time it was, how long until dawn, when this place would be bustling with people who could help her.

She had pepper spray in her pocketbook. But where was her pocketbook?

Where were the video cameras, the web cams? They must be everywhere. Security guards must be monitoring every corner of the airport, every hour of the day—like God up in heaven.

But maybe God only monitored the main public areas—near the ticket counters and the gates and baggage claim. Maybe He didn't watch the long twisting corridors and passageways of the airport.

"Can I help you, ma'am?" the stranger asked, his voice muffled by his scarf.

Moments later she was sitting, crouched on the floor. How did she get there? She was telling this stranger everything that she had said to Matt, like it was a fixed speech she had prepared; except this time she emphasized that she had finally made up her mind, that she was not going to Arizona—not today, not tomorrow, not ever. Boston was her home. Tom was her husband in fact, if not in name. She loved him. She loved her children. After all their years of marriage, she was not going to leave him, not over Meeghan, not over anyone else, if there was anyone else. And there wasn't. She was sure of it. He loved her as much as she loved him. Forever. Period. God bless this storm, this wonderful storm that had prevented her from making a terrible mistake. She had to get home quickly. Tom and the children must know about the cancellations. They must be worried. She had to hug them and kiss them and reassure them that she loved them and that she would never, ever leave them again.

She saw light reflecting off metal a moment before she felt a blade at her throat.

23 ~ Recovery

When Alex knocked on Tom's door at two in the morning, Tom was in bed, but neither awake nor asleep. He had had a few beers, feeling sorry for himself—betrayed by Marge who was leaving him, and betrayed by Alex who had made it easy for her to do so.

Alex explained that he had checked online, and Marge's flight was cancelled. He had tried to reach her on her cell phone, but it was turned off. Then he had tried calling the airline and the airport, but both were closed for the night.

Even after a mug of coffee, Tom was groggy. It took a while for the words, repeated several times, to sink in.

Patti was frantic. She sensed that something was wrong. She didn't like this Arizona business and had tried to talk Marge out of it. Now she had called 911 and gotten the runaround that no one can be presumed missing until they've been gone for forty-eight hours. Then she had called a taxi. She was now bundled up and waiting for the taxi to arrive. Tom and Alex would go with her. Not that she had any idea where to look for Marge at the airport, and of course, they wouldn't be able to get past security and go to the gate area, where she might be asleep on a chair or on the floor, waiting for a morning flight. But Patti insisted that once they were at the airport they must be able to get someone to check the gate areas, and they could check the public areas themselves. They had to do something. The airport at night was as dangerous as the Common at night. And they all knew how dangerous that was.

Patti's panic-mode was contagious. By the time they got to the airport, both Alex and Tom were as fired up as she was. While Patti pleaded with a guard at security, who insisted that he couldn't leave his post, Tom and Alex sprinted in different directions past all the empty check-in counters of Terminal B and then through other corridors leading to the rest of the airport complex.

Tom found Marge in a pool of blood in an enclosed passageway that led over the highway to Central Parking. This time 911 responded quickly.

There was a long cut on her throat. It had narrowly missed an artery. The EMTs speculated that whoever did this had wanted to kill her, then changed his mind. There were blood-stained paper towels on the ground around her, as if someone had tried, with pressure, to stop the bleeding. Maybe he waited until he thought the bleeding had stopped, then he left.

She was fully clothed.

They said she could have been lying there for an hour or two. They thought that she would make it. But if she hadn't been found until dawn, she might have bled to death.

The EMTs took her to Mass. General by ambulance. She was in shock. A breathalyzer test showed a high alcohol concentration. At her weight, it would take half a dozen martinis to get to that level.

Tom stayed with her. He told the EMTs he was her husband, and they let him ride with her in the ambulance. At the hospital, to avoid falling into a bureaucratic trap that would keep him away, he said once again that he was her husband. No one asked him for ID.

The emergency room staff concluded that she had not been raped. The police thought it was a random act of violence. Whoever did it probably got a thrill from inflicting fear and pain, but was conflicted enough to change his mind and try to save her.

Marge, not yet conscious, mumbled in delirium. Tom caught words about corridors, about a maze, wanting to find a way out. He wasn't sure whether she was talking about the airport or her life. He couldn't make sense of it. He had a hard enough time trying to decipher her theories when she was conscious and alert.

She muttered about guilt and infidelity and "thou shalt not commit adultery." She mentioned Zeke. She mentioned Jack. She mentioned Tom. She mentioned Meeghan. She even mentioned someone named Matt, who Tom had never heard of before.

Tom stayed with her in the Emergency Room until noon the next day when they moved her, still unconscious, to Intensive Care. And he stayed with her there until she regained consciousness, and they moved her to a semi-private room. Once there, Patti and Alex could visit, and Tom could go home and get some sleep.

She answered the doctors' questions and acknowledged the presence of her visitors. But she didn't want to say anything about what had happened to her.

The police had no fingerprints, no witnesses, no clues of any kind.

When she went home a few days later, she was quiet and withdrawn, and the others left her alone when she wanted to be alone. They skipped Thanksgiving.

That weekend, she asked Tom to rent all the old Meg Ryan movies, and they watched them non-stop, day and night.

Then they talked softly together on the sofa, hour after hour, sorting through everything that had happened since she moved in.

At first, Marge presumed that Zeke was responsible for their problems, that he had orchestrated everything from a distance, like Alex would have been able to do.

Then other clues started falling into place—no, it wasn't Zeke. It was someone local.

Someone had posed as a friend to Jack and fed him stories to make him believe that Marge was unfaithful. That same person had pointed Jack to the web page and had prompted him to confront her at the apartment and try to get her to leave Tom.

Also, someone had told Diane things she couldn't have known from the web cam. Someone had broken into her house at the Cape and heard the message on her answering machine and thereby had learned the new phone number and then erased the message. That same person had befriended Diane and pointed her to the web page and had prompted her to call Tom and get him to drive down, and then to go to Boston herself.

No. They were getting paranoid. Either one of those stories was a stretch. And both at once would be an impossible coincidence. And there was no motive for anyone to have gone to all that trouble.

But, in any case, the airport attack was unrelated. It was a random act of violence—like Patti's attack on the Common and the couple who were stalking Marge. Living in today's world was like trying to navigate through the asteroid belt—there were too many random risks for you to avoid all of them. But you couldn't let that stop you. Once hit, you had to pick yourself up and get going again.

24 ~ Ezekiel's Wife

Tom suggested that they all go out to dinner—his treat, at another North End Italian restaurant. It would be good to get out of the apartment. And the streets and stores were all lit up for Christmas. They could enjoy walking down Newbury Street with all its decorations, then take a cab.

Marge fetched her coat and checked the pockets for her mittens. That was when she found the note. That stalker girl must have slipped it in her pocket as she got into the cab to go to the airport.

The paper had been soaked by the rain, and very little was legible. "Ezekiel's Wife" it began.

Marge froze and showed it to the others. "That's ridiculous," she protested. "I'm not and never was Ezekiel's wife. And I certainly never will be. Not now. Not after all this. Why would that person think such a thing? Unless Zeke put her up to it. Unless Zeke paid her and her friend to harass me and drive me out of here. God," she screamed. "Enough. I've had enough!"

Alex said, "There's a number near the bottom. Ten digits. Looks like a phone number. I don't recognize the area code. Maybe it's a cell phone."

"No," Marge protested. "Don't call it. Don't do what she wants, what Zeke wants me to do. Keep them away. Keep them away from me."

She retreated to her room, but in the background she could hear Alex on the phone, talking to someone, inviting someone to come to the apartment and sort this out.

When the girl and her companion arrived half an hour later, Patti tried to coax Marge out of her room. But Marge insisted on sitting on the sofa, while the others sat at the kitchen table.

The girl was short—no more than five foot one. She looked about the same age as Alex. Marge imagined that, next to Zeke, she would look like a child.

"Before we say anything else," Marge insisted, "let's get one thing straight—I am not Ezekiel's wife."

"Of course not," the girl replied with a puzzled look. "I am."

"You are what?"

"My name is Emily. And this is my brother Eli. Ezekiel and I got married about two years ago."

"Do I know you?" asked Marge, in disbelief.

"You wouldn't remember me. But I remember you. I was five when you ran away. But I've seen so many photos of you and heard so much about you, I feel I've known you all my life."

"But you're not old enough to be his wife. You could be his daughter."

"Yes," she admitted, tears welling in her eyes. "It's not easy when you love someone who's older. Here he was my first love, and I'd do anything to make him mine forever, to mature with him, to grow old with him. And here he was already so experienced and scarred by heartbreak. I had to be careful what I said for fear of triggering the wrong memories and pushing him away from me."

"Land mines," Tom muttered, nodding his head as if he understood.

"What?" asked Emily. "No, I didn't say land mines. Nothing like that. Nothing that sounded anything like that. Land mines'? What could that mean? No, we had just heard from the doctor, as I had feared, that I couldn't have babies. And I was telling Ezekiel that we should adopt, and not adopt just one or two. We should get three or four or even more. We had plenty of room. We could fix the attic up and make bedrooms for the kids up there. I wanted to get his mind off what couldn't be and get him thinking about our future together. So I told him, 'Let's go up to the attic now and take a look and plan. Let's go up to the attic together.' Then he screamed and stormed out of the house. The next I heard from him was a phone call from him from Boston."

Emily explained that he had said he needed to find Marge, that Marge was his "true wife" and that he would return with her or not at all.

Apparently, he believed that Emily was barren as a punishment from God. Marge was his true wife. But he must find and win back his true wife.

Marge remembered what she had said out loud at the airport to the stranger, just before the attack—that she had narrowly missed making a terrible mistake, that Tom was the love her life and always would be.

According to Emily, Ezekiel had made no secret about where he was going and what he was doing. He had called Emily every few days to report on his progress and to give her instructions for the help so they could keep the farm going.

He was proud and happy when Marge left Jack a few months back. Then when Marge moved in with Tom, he started making elaborate plans. He tracked down Diane at the Cape and became her friend and learned details about Tom from her and prompted her to try to get back together with Tom.

The attack on Patti in the park wasn't Ezekiel. Emily was sure of that. Soon after that he broke down when talking to her on the phone. He cried and cursed and screamed. The web cam had been found. And the cops would be after him for that, and might even blame him for the attack, what with all the stuff he had been doing, all the calls, and the people he had talked to who knew Tom and Marge. There was no way he could talk his way out of that mess.

That was the last Emily had heard from him. He had closed his cell phone account. He had moved out of the room he had been renting in Cambridge. She and her brother came out here to find him and bring him home.

She just wanted him back. She hoped he would drop all the plotting and just talk to Marge. Then he would realize that she wasn't the same person he had loved seventeen years ago. He would exorcise this ghost of the past that had been haunting him, and he would be able to come home. He and Emily could start together again fresh.

Patti explained to Emily, gently and compassionately, that while Zeke was probably not responsible for the attack on her in the Common, he may have attacked Marge at the airport.

Emily hadn't heard about that. She listened quietly, trembling, as Patti gave her version of that event.

Then Emily protested that no, Ezekiel could never do that. He was a godly, tenderhearted, generous man.

Stretched out on the sofa, staring at the ceiling, Marge tuned out Emily's defense. She felt like a kaleidoscope shaken again and again—her memories kept falling into one new pattern after another.

She had begun to accept the airport attack as a random act of violence, just as Patti's must have been. But now she understood that the man hadn't been a stranger, that it had been deliberate, that Zeke had been stalking her, hovering near her for months, trying to manipulate the thoughts and feelings of those around her, and plotting to get her back to Arizona, or, failing that, making sure that no one else had her.

A random attack by a stranger she could live with.

But attempted murder, her murder, premeditated by someone who was still at large, who still had just as much reason to kill her as before—that shook her.

She felt her essential self shrinking in fear as when she had felt the knife at her throat.

She needed to be alone

She went up the ladder to the attic. She needed to be alone.

She would go to the hiding place. That was what it was for—the ultimate refuge.

She had only been there once before. She hadn't wanted to go along the ramparts. Tom's talk of his vertigo had spooked her. She preferred to stay away from heights. But she couldn't let that stop her now. She wouldn't let herself be afraid. She would never be afraid of anything again.

But as she climbed through the window to the hiding place, the beam of a bright flashlight struck her in the face, and after a moment, when her eyes adjusted, she saw near the window Pru's dressmaker's model, and, in the far corner, light reflecting off a knife blade and Zeke, crouched, ready to leap at her.

25 ~ Last Shot

Patti understood that Marge would want to be alone. But she needed to talk to her about the implications of this latest revelation.

She left Tom and Alex with Emily and Emily's brother in the kitchen and scrambled up the ladder.

From the open window, she knew that Marge must have headed to the hiding place. That was good. It was a sign that she was dealing with her fears—old ones as well as new ones—that she would cope, that she would pull herself together and get on with her life.

But they needed to recalibrate, to decide what they could and should do for protection, until this monster was arrested by the police. And surely that would be soon now that they knew who he was and knew where he had been hanging out in recent months. She wanted to be sure that Marge agreed with her about how to proceed before she called the police. It would only be a few minutes, and then she'd leave Marge to her quiet and solitude.

Though the sky was overcast and starless, the lights of Back Bay, of the Prudential Center and the John Hancock Tower glittered brilliantly through a chilled fog. She paused a moment, leaning over the wall, remembering that day, less than three months ago when she and Alex first came to this building; and, from up here, Marge and Tom, watched them approach.

Then through the traffic noise and the distant siren of an ambulance, she heard what sounded like a muffled scream.

As she turned the corner, she saw a moving beam of light through the window of the hiding place. But Marge didn't have a flashlight. In the hiding place, there was a light switch by the window, behind the dressmaker's model. But this wasn't a stationary light. Rapidly moving shadows played on the brick wall of the neighboring building.

Patti almost turned back to get Alex and Tom. Then her instinct drew her forward, instinct born of experience—if Marge was in real danger, there was no time to waste.

Old words raced through her head. "Sometimes life is like an attic. What you want and need is right there if you could just find it. If you could just remember...'"

She moved quickly and quietly to the window.

A man, with his back to the window, had Marge pinned to the floor. She was struggling to hold back his knife.

Without thinking, Patti reached inside the window to the pocket of the violet outfit on the dressmaker's model, and in a single motion she grasped the derringer, aimed, and pulled the trigger. It clicked.

The attacker jumped up—he was huge, far taller than Tom. He spun around, knife extended in front him, and lunged at Patti at the window.

She screamed, pulled back the hammer, and squeezed again.

He collapsed, blood spurting from his chest. He smashed into the dressmaker's model, which shattered, scattering old broken bones across the floor of the hiding place.

***

The medical examiner took away the bones, along with the fresh body. The bones looked at least a hundred years old. Of course, the present residents wouldn't know anything about them.

Epilogue

Nearly six months after it all began, after weeks of snow and freezing rain, on Mardi Gras, the sun shone bright and the temperature reached a record high, creating the illusion of mid-summer.

In full sartorial splendor, the gang of four walked from Fairfield Street to an Italian restaurant in the North End. Much of the way, they followed the Freedom Trail, focusing on the bright blue sky, while avoiding patches of soot-sprinkled snow and ice at their feet.

Alex wore black jeans, black turtle-neck sweater, black snow hat, even black leather gloves.

Tom wore Alex's 1930's gangster outfit.

Patti carried a parasol and wore Pru's violet outfit, with full-length skirt and straw hat, and sneakers for comfort.

Marge got into the spirit of the occasion, donning short shorts, with bare midriff and removable belly-button ring, and bright blue hair.

Over a Sicilian pizza, with everything on it, Tom lamented, "All that time in the gym, all those lessons and my bionic leg, and I was useless. And you, Alex, with all your cyber-sleuth skills, you had no clue what the real threat was."

"You're right, brother," Alex put on his Robert Parker/Hawk imitation again. "All this talent and all these skills are going to waste. It's high time we started that detective business you were talking about."

"Sure, Alex. Sure. With Patti here as our on-staff femme fatale."

"Definitely fatale," Alex added.

"And what about me?" asked Marge.

"Remember Susan?" Tom asked back.

"Susan?"

"Spenser's girlfriend in the Robert Parker novels. She's a psychologist. You're a social psychologist."

"No way. Sign me up as CEO. This business of yours needs at least one adult."

About the Author

Richard lives in Milford, CT, where he writes fiction, poetry, and essays full-time. He worked for DEC, the minicomputer company, as writer and Internet evangelist. He graduated from Yale with a major in English, went to Yale grad school in Comparative Literature, and earned an MA from the U. of Mass. at Amherst. At Yale, he had creative writing courses with Robert Penn Warren and Joseph Heller. His published works include: *Parallel Lives*, *Beyond the 4th Door*, *Nevermind*, *Breeze*, *Shakespeare's Twin Sister*, *To Gether Tales*, and *Echoes from the Attic* (from All Things That Matter Press), *Grandad Jokes*, *If Not, Why Not?* (essays), *The Lizard of Oz and Other Stories* (from Booklocker), *The Name of Hero* (historical novel), *Ethiopia Through Russian Eyes* (translation from Russian), and pioneering books about Internet business. His personal web site is seltzerbooks.com

Ethel Kaiden has been a speech writer for CEO's of major corporations including Schlumberger, Digital Equipment Corporation and Wang Laboratories. She has written prize winning television advertising commercials and public service campaigns and has helped name products and companies. Ethel is the daughter of Jack Weinstock Tony Award author of Pullitzer Prize winning Broadway musical " How To Succeed in Business Without Really Trying" for which he won a Tony Award and Screen Writers award. He co-authored mystery/comedy play Catch Me if You Can and major Television shows to numerous to mention. Ethel has written several short stories and assisted her father with comic special material. She was a Public Relations executive and Press Agent before co-authoring "Echoes From The Attic".

9 798987 129647